Full Throttle

Lisa R. Schoolcraft

Full Throttle

Lisa R. Schoolcraft

Table of Contents

Chapter 1

Laura Lucas did not want to get out of bed. She did not want to go down to Axel's Motors and do any sort of public relations for the new manager. Why? He was a felon. A convicted felon!

She pulled the duvet over her head. Then she rolled over and hit snooze for the second time. When the alarm went off again, she knew she couldn't delay the day any longer.

Today was the grand opening of the new service station. Axel's Motors was named for Axel Lynch, the recently paroled convicted felon.

The only reason Axel had the job as manager of the business was because his stepbrother, Kyle Quitman, had purchased an old service station and renovated it. No one would have hired him straight out of prison for this position. She hoped Kyle knew what he was doing.

Laura did public relations for Kyle, CEO of Black Kat Investors. And now she was going to have to do public relations work for Axel.

Laura wasn't going to work with Axel this morning without her Cuban coffee. She put on her robe and went into the kitchen of her Buckhead penthouse. She began the process — and it was a process — of making Cuban coffee in the cafetera. She whisked up the froth before she put sugar and milk in the strong, earthy coffee.

She sipped it while buttering a flaky croissant, sitting at her small dining table just off the kitchen. Her home office's desk was in front of that. From her desk, she could work in her penthouse and look out onto a portion of Buckhead's skyline.

More residential towers were going up, Laura noticed. Soon there wouldn't be a square inch of space undeveloped in Buckhead, a luxe area in the city of Atlanta.

The joke in the commercial real estate world was that the construction crane was the unofficial bird of Atlanta. Every time she drove down Peachtree Road, she noticed more buildings going up.

This March morning, she finished her first cup of coffee, then made another before washing her cup and her plate. She showered, got dressed, and headed down to her car.

Laura had thought about what she would wear to the service station, which had been completely renovated, so for now, it wasn't a dirty, filthy shop. She could wear something nice.

Laura decided on dark gray dress slacks, a burgundy sweater, and her stiletto heels. Laura was slightly taller than five feet, but in her heels, she could stand nearly five foot three inches.

A petite woman, she needed that height compared to Axel, who was almost a foot taller than she. Axel's muscular frame included arm tattoos. She imagined he had other tattoos, but she didn't want to think about where those were on his body. He disgusted her.

Laura pulled into Axel's Motors in the Lindbergh area, which was still a part of Buckhead, but to Laura's mind, it wasn't the nicest part of Buckhead. Lindbergh was more industrial. A train station was nearby. Truth be told, Axel's Motors service station was nicer than the properties that surrounded it.

She arrived well before the shop would open. Axel's battered pickup truck wasn't out front. She'd asked him to park it where it couldn't be seen by the media and new clients.

Laura had invited some local politicians, including Sam Massell, the "honorary mayor of Buckhead," TV stations, local newspapers, some bloggers, and social media influencers.

She found Axel inside the lobby of the service station, pacing nervously. He was in dark gray pants and matching jacket with a black shirt. The jacket appeared to be a bit too small for him.

"When does Kyle get here?" she asked him.

"No, good morning, Axel? How did you sleep last night?"

"Good morning, Axel," Laura huffed. "Satisfied? When does Kyle arrive?"

"Good morning to you. Kyle said he'd be here by nine o'clock. Want some coffee? I'll make a pot."

"I've had my coffee."

"I have some fresh donuts on the counter, next to the coffee maker."

"I've had my breakfast."

"You are just a breath of fresh air today, aren't you?"

"I told you. I don't like you," Laura said, bluntly. "Now memorize this sheet," she said, handing him a one-page sheet of letter-sized paper.

"What's this?" he asked, taking it from her.

"It's your new life."

"My new life? What's wrong with the one I have?"

"That one didn't really work out for you, now did it?"

"So, you created a new life? And I'm supposed to memorize this right now?"

"I think we both know the answer to that."

Axel began to read what was listed on the sheet.

"I got my business degree online?"

"Well, we can't say you got it in prison, now can we? That's a sure way to have no customers, ever."

"And I have a wife and two kids to support?"

"Sure, why not?"

"Laura, I'm divorced. My wife divorced me when I went to prison. We never had kids."

"Can't say I blame her. Go ahead and say you're divorced. That's OK. Maybe some of the women will be sympathetic to you. If you were divorced, with kids, it would have been better."

Axel tossed the sheet of paper back at Laura. "You're a piece of work, you know that?"

"You just need a better resume, Axel. You can't let anyone know where you've been the past five to ten."

"It was four years. Good behavior."

Laura snorted a laugh.

"Why are you such a bitch?"

"Why are you such a felon?"

"Look, I paid my dues, OK? I'm out and I'm making a fresh start here in Atlanta."

3

Kyle entered the front door to Laura and Axel arguing. Kyle clapped his hands to get their attention.

"Children! Children! Am I going to have to separate you and put you in time out?"

"I am not a child, Kyle! I'm trying to get Axel to memorize this script so he's ready for the media attention today," Laura said, glaring at Axel.

"Oh sure, throw me under the bus. Kyle, Laura gave this to me minutes ago. She didn't let me know she was inventing a whole new life for me. I can't memorize this so quickly. And really, why should I? I'm not ashamed of my life."

"You should be!" Laura cut in. "If you mention prison, the media will pounce on that, and this place will be closed. No customers will come here — ever."

"Alright! Alright!" Kyle said, putting his hands up. "Just stop it. Laura, can you condense this page to just a few paragraphs? Something that's easier to remember?"

Laura frowned. "I'll need to type it up. Let me go get my laptop. Do you have a printer here?"

"Yes," Axel said.

Laura went to her car and got her laptop out of the trunk. She returned to the lobby and sat down at the receptionist's desk and typed up a shorter version of Axel's new life. She stuck to the very basics.

"Where's the printer? My laptop isn't recognizing it."

"Let me go turn it on," Axel said, disappearing into a small side room. He came back out and Laura asked for the Wi-Fi password, then found the printer and printed out the new version.

Axel pulled it off the printer and nodded. "I can work with this."

As he walked past Laura, she inhaled. "What is that scent? Is that Old Spice? My God, my grandfather wore that."

"Cut me some slack, bitch," Axel shot back. "Not everyone can afford that fancy shit you wear."

"Hey, hey, hey! No name-calling," Kyle said through gritted teeth. "I have no patience for either one of you today. I need you both to be on your best behavior."

The media began arriving shortly before the 11 a.m. ribbon cutting. It was mostly community newspapers. Laura also hired a freelance photographer, Joann Angelini, to take photos as well. Laura would send out a press release with several photos of the event to those who weren't in attendance.

She also found a Facebook group of car enthusiasts in metro Atlanta and invited them, too. Why not? She needed a good crowd of people to show up.

Laura would also send the release and photos to several social media influencers. She was hoping they would post to Twitter, Instagram, and Facebook with the hashtags #AxelsMotors #newbusiness #carcaredoneright.

Laura could see Axel being interviewed by a few reporters and walked over to listen. He kept stammering, not remembering his "new life." He made some mistakes, which one reporter questioned. Then he froze and stopped talking. Laura thought he looked like a deer in the headlights.

Laura stepped in when she saw Axel getting frustrated.

"What I think Mr. Lynch meant to say, is he got his degree online while he was working full-time as a mechanic," she interrupted.

She sensed Axel relax when she took over. The reporter kept asking questions to Axel, but Laura kept answering for him.

Then Laura gave the reporter her business card and told her to contact her if she had any more questions.

As she turned away, she heard Axel whisper, "Thanks. I don't like the media."

"Neither do I, but it's a necessary evil. Why don't you go stand over by some of those lift things and let our photographer get some publicity shots of you. Get some of the techs in there, too."

"I don't have to answer any questions from her, do I?"

"No, just listen when she wants you to stand a certain way. Then just smile and look pretty in your suit."

Axel grunted as he let Joann lead him away for the publicity shots. He motioned for some of the techs to join him.

Kyle came up to Laura's shoulder. "Thank you for saving him."

"I should have done more media training with him, but it's just for today. I didn't expect him to freeze like that."

"I should have realized he probably doesn't like the media, given his background."

"Was there a trial?"

"No, he pleaded guilty right away. He knew what he'd done was wrong."

"So why did he do it?" Laura asked.

"You'll have to ask him that. He's never told me."

"My brother started dealing drugs because he liked being in with a gang. Made him feel important. It's not like he needed the money. My parents gave him everything."

Kyle looked at Laura. "Oh, I didn't know that."

Suddenly, Laura realized what she'd said. She'd revealed too much of her personal life. "Well, he's dead, so it didn't really work out for him."

"I'm very sorry to hear that."

"Don't be. Just be thankful your stepbrother is out of it now." Laura paused. "He is out of it now, right?"

"He's told me he's out and I believe him."

"Are you making him take random drug tests? You probably should."

"His parole officer will make him do that."

"That's good."

"But Laura, it's not like that. He never used drugs."

"Neither did my brother."

Kyle was quiet after that.

Axel came back into the lobby with Joann. She started showing him some of the shots through the back of her digital camera. Then she showed some of the photos to Laura.

"I think we've got some photos you'll really like," she said to Laura. "I'll send you a contact sheet and you tell me what you want. I will send them over in a zip file. The images will be big. You can use them however you want."

"Fabulous. I appreciate it."

Laura, with Kyle's blessing, had ordered a catered box lunch for the employees at the service station that day. "Don't get too used to it," she said, smiling. "We won't be doing this every day."

Most of the technicians were young men. They attacked the free food. She was glad she'd ordered seven extra sandwiches. She felt sure there would be none left.

"Where's your lunch?" Axel asked, holding a box that said it held a roast beef sandwich.

"I'll have one of the vegetarian ones. I figured those would be unpopular."

"I'll get it for you."

But Axel returned empty-handed. "I think someone ate all of them."

"I ordered two of them. The Caprese sandwich."

"Oh. I think there is one left. I thought that was some sort of Italian meat. It didn't say vegetarian."

Axel walked back to the long table they had set up in the lobby and brought back the boxed lunch, handing it to Laura.

"We can sit over there," he said, pointing with his boxed lunch to an empty card table with three chairs around it.

Axel pulled out a chair for Laura, then took off his jacket, putting it around his own chair.

Laura reluctantly walked over and sat down. Axel bowed his head and began to pray before he opened his lunch.

"Oh God, don't tell me you found religion while you were in prison," Laura said softly, so she couldn't be overheard.

"Is that such a bad thing?" Axel asked, pulling out his sandwich and putting it on the wax paper it had been wrapped in.

"I mean, it's so cliché," Laura said, folding her hands as if in prayer. "Help me get out of prison, Jesus, and I'll go straight," she mimicked. "Then you are out, forget about your newfound religion, and go right back to a life of crime."

"It's not that way with me. I take comfort in religion. It helped me through some bad times in prison. And, for your information, Princess, I'm never going back to a life of crime or prison again."

Laura arched an eyebrow.

"Don't give me that look, Princess. It's the truth."

"Stop calling me that!"

"What? Princess? Should I call you a diva instead? Because you act like one."

7

Laura made a face at Axel.

"Be careful. My mother always said your face could get stuck like that."

Laura stood up. "I think I'll eat my lunch over there." She put her sandwich back in the box and took it to another table.

Laura sat down with some other technicians. She gave them a big smile and asked, "Mind if I join you?"

"Boss man giving you trouble?" one tech asked.

"Let's just say he's not a great conversationalist. He's rude and obnoxious."

The tech gave Laura a toothy grin. "He's kind of a jackass."

"Careful," said another tech, poking his friend with his elbow. "He'll hear you."

"I don't care. I think he knows he's a jackass and he doesn't care if we know it."

"Well, let's not talk about him," Laura said, watching Axel stare at her and the men she was sitting with. "How long have you all been in the automotive industry?"

"I'm just a grease monkey," the first tech laughed. "I'm not in the automotive industry."

Laura gave a little laugh. "Oh, sorry, mister grease monkey. How long have you been in this circus?"

That brought guffaws from the table.

"Been doing this since I was a teenager. My father was really into cars. We restored a 1968 Mustang together."

The other men at the table oohed and aahed at the statement. Laura could tell they were all just young boys at heart dreaming of classic muscle cars.

"I bet that was a sweet ride when you were done," she said.

The tech pulled out his phone and showed the table a picture of the restored blue Ford. It looked great.

"Now that's a sweet looking car," the second tech said. "You're a lucky son of a bitch."

"Well, it's my dad's car. He's the one driving it around."

"Here in Atlanta?" she asked. "I'd be afraid someone would steal it."

"No, my parents live in Nahunta," he said, pronouncing it Nay-hunna. Laura guessed Nahunta was his hometown.

"Where's that?" Laura asked.

"South Georgia."

Laura nodded like she knew where that was, but she had no idea. If it wasn't in Buckhead or the surrounding metro Atlanta counties, she imagined other parts of Georgia were all cotton fields and peanut farms. Farmers in denim overalls without a full set of teeth. Wasn't Jimmy Carter a peanut farmer? She remembered he had a big toothy smile.

She realized the first tech was still talking to her about the car. She could almost picture the guy getting a hard-on about the car.

Laura just kept nodding. She stopped paying attention to what any of the techs were saying when it came to anything about cars. She just knew she liked to drive her Mercedes-Benz.

Chapter 2

Laura headed home, her feet aching in the car. She had taken her shoes off to drive home and wished she had booked a massage for tomorrow.

She'd worked her tail off all day, walking back and forth on the service station's concrete floor. Now her feet and back were paying for it.

Laura called Craig Dawson on her way home. Craig, a commercial real estate broker, was married, but they'd been having an on-again-off-again affair that was currently very much on.

"Craig, I'm done with my work for today," Laura said into his voicemail. "Want to have dinner with me tonight? And dessert back at my place?"

She walked through her front door, her shoes in her hand. She could feel the blisters rising on her toes.

Laura turned and set the security system on her door.

Her condo building, with a parking gate and doors that opened with keycards, was very secure. But Laura slept better at night with her extra security, which had been installed without her condo association's consent or knowledge. A friend of a friend in the military had installed it.

She sat down and began rubbing her feet. She then went into her bathroom to get some bandages to put on her blisters.

Laura went back into her kitchen to get a glass of wine. She was hoping Craig would drive when they went out to dinner.

She finally got a call from Craig. He couldn't have dinner with her that night. He was committed to a charity dinner with his wife.

"Well, what am I supposed to do for dinner tonight?" she asked him.

"Laura, order some takeout, or go out by yourself."

"But I wanted to go out with you," she replied.

"We can go out tomorrow."

"It's Friday night. Can you get away from your wife to take me out?"

"I'll tell her I have a client dinner and you and I will go out."

"OK. Take me somewhere nice."

"Of course."

"In Buckhead."

"Maybe somewhere a little further out where we won't be seen."

"Craig, I want to go somewhere nice."

"We can go up to Alpharetta. There's a good steakhouse up there. I can drive my Porsche up 400."

"There are good steakhouses in Buckhead, you know."

"No, Alpharetta. We won't be recognized. See you tomorrow, Laura."

Laura hung up and pouted. She didn't expect that she'd have to get her own dinner tonight and she really didn't want to drive up to Alpharetta to get a steak tomorrow. But if Craig was paying for it, she'd have to go along for the ride.

By now she'd had three glasses of white wine, so she didn't want to drive for dinner. She decided to order Chinese delivery. Grand China in Buckhead delivered.

She decided on some dumplings and the roast duck with plum sauce. She knew that was more food than she really wanted, but she'd have leftovers for lunch the next day. She certainly wasn't buying lunch for everyone at the service station tomorrow.

The front desk concierge called Laura when the food arrived and said it was on its way up. Laura unlocked her front door and waited by the elevator.

Friday morning Laura attempted to put on her stilettos but found it impossible. Instead, she reached into the back of her closet for the boots she had purchased in Napa Valley last summer.

She wore her designer jeans and tucked them into the boots, pairing the outfit with a teal-colored cotton blouse. She wore a beige long fringe vest over the shirt. If she could have worn her slippers back to the service station she would have.

When she walked into the service station, Axel was already there. He seemed taller to her. Then she realized without her heels, he was almost a foot taller.

"Good morning, sunshine," Axel said. "Where are the heels?"

Laura was not going to admit she had blisters on her feet from yesterday's inappropriate shoe choice.

"Oh, just mixing up my look today. I wanted to fit in with all the blue-collar workers."

"Blue-collar workers? You couldn't fit in with the working class if you tried."

"You are an asshole. Do you know that?"

"I've been told," Axel said, taking a sip of coffee. He did not offer a cup to Laura this morning. If she wanted it, she was going to have to ask.

Laura walked over to the coffee maker and pulled a Styrofoam cup from the tower of cups next to it. She poured a cup. "Where's the sugar and cream?"

Axel pointed to two cylinders next to the coffee maker.

"This crap?" she asked, picking up powdered creamer. She dumped the coffee in the trash.

"Sorry, Princess. I'll try to have cream and sugar for you next time."

"I'll just make a quick run to Starbucks."

"Don't go now. I don't want you to leave me alone with those piranhas."

"Who? The media? They came yesterday."

"Who's coming today then?"

"I've got a radio station going to do a live broadcast during afternoon drive time."

"Does anyone listen to the radio anymore?"

"Not many, which is why I got them so cheap. It's a country station. I figured the audience would have pickup trucks and other big vehicles that would need servicing."

"What time will they be here?"

"They are starting at two o'clock and they will broadcast for two hours."

"But I don't have to say anything?"

"They are going to interview you several times during the broadcast."

"I need you to be right here when that happens. Don't go anywhere."

"OK. But I'm going to get some Starbucks right now. I'll be back in just a few minutes."

Laura left and returned almost an hour later. She'd nearly finished her coffee.

"Where were you?" Axel raged. He was pacing the station's lobby, the radio station techs setting up the remote broadcast in one corner of the station.

"I went for coffee!"

"Where? To Buckhead?"

"Yes. I went to the one near my condo. They know my order."

"The radio people showed up early, Laura. They wanted to do an interview right away. I wouldn't let them until you got back."

"I'm here now, so let's get the interview started. It will be fine."

The auto technicians were jamming to the country music and asking questions of and flirting with the female deejay. Laura walked up to the mobile broadcast station and asked the deejay if she was ready to do the interview with Axel now.

"Give me about 10 minutes," she said, removing her headset. "I want to do it after the sponsor break."

Laura walked away as the deejay put her headset back on and said, "That's the latest hit song from Lady Antebellum. It's rising in the charts. Next up is a duet by Tim McGraw and Faith Hill, 'The Rest of Our Life.' And when we come back from break, we'll hear from the man behind Axel's Motors here in Lindbergh."

Laura turned to Axel and spoke softly, "Remember the script. Don't stray from it or say anything off the top of your head. If you forget something, turn to me. I'll break in and answer for you."

Axel looked nervous but shook his head in agreement.

When the song was nearly over, the deejay motioned Axel to step closer and put a headset on. Axel looked at Laura and panicked. She put her hand on his arm and gave it a little squeeze. His arm felt like a rock, she thought.

When the commercial break was over, the deejay began asking Axel about his experience as a mechanic. Next, she asked why he wanted to open Axel's Motors.

"I think people are scared of trusting their mechanic," he said. "And they shouldn't be. We're here to be honest with you. If you need a new transmission, we'll tell you. But if you don't need a new transmission, we'll tell you that too."

The deejay cut away from the interview, then began the songs again.

"Wow," Axel said, removing his headset. "That was easier than I thought."

"You did well. I'll ask her if there will be any more interview questions."

Laura walked over to the deejay and asked if she was done with the interviews.

"I'd like to do two more. The first one will be in a half-hour and then another an hour from now. That will close out my remote broadcast."

"OK. We'll be in the lobby. Text me and we'll be right out," Laura said, handing the woman her business card.

The deejay nodded and broke in to introduce the next song.

Laura walked with Axel to the lobby. "You did fine out there. Just keep it up."

"I didn't have to lie about my past with those questions," he said bitterly.

"Hey, I'm being honest with you that if you mention that you were in prison, you can kiss this service station goodbye."

"I know that."

"Start memorizing and living your new life. Look at it as an opportunity for a clean slate."

"It must be great to be you."

"It is great to be me."

"No, I mean you provide me with a sheet of paper with a new life on it and expect that what you've handed me will make my life better."

"Well, won't it?"

"I can't live a lie, Laura."

"You most certainly don't have to live a lie, Axel. Just begin living your new life right now."

"That's not so easy."

Laura frowned. "Why isn't it so easy? Are you dealing again?"

"Absolutely not!" he shouted.

Several of the techs turned and stared.

"Keep your voice down," Laura hissed.

"I'm not dealing," Axel said under his breath. "I'm not. I told you I'm not going back to prison."

"Well then learn to lead your new life!"

Laura's phone binged with a text message. The deejay was ready for another interview.

"She wants us back out there. Take some deep breaths, Axel. Calm down. I can't have you going out there angry."

Axel glared at Laura. "I'm fine. I don't need your hippy-dippy breathing techniques."

"Suit yourself."

Laura and Axel walked out to the remote broadcast and the deejay handed Axel a headset. He put it on and took a deep breath.

"And we're back with Axel Lynch, owner of Axel's Motors," the deejay said. "So, you've told us about being a mechanic, but tell me how you became a businessman."

"Well, I'm not the owner. I'm the manager. And I'm lucky to have some investors who believe in me," Axel said with confidence. "It's allowed me this opportunity to open Axel's Motors, a service station you can trust with your car."

Laura smiled at his statement. He was doing great, she thought.

"And do you have any business experience? Did you own a shop before this one?"

Axel started to answer, then froze. "I, ah, got my business degree online."

'Oh. That's great. What online program did you get your degree from?"

Axel couldn't remember what Laura's paper had said, so he said the one he used in prison. "Oh, it was Adams State University."

"That's great. That's not one I've heard of, but that's great. We'll be back one more time with Axel Lynch in about a half-hour."

Axel took off the headset to see Laura fuming.

She grabbed him by his arm and pulled him through the lobby and into his office.

"What the hell? You didn't follow the script! What's Adams State University?"

"I blanked out. It's the program I used at the prison."

"Shit!"

"Did I screw up?" he asked, puzzled.

"I don't know, Axel. I thought you would remember the University of Phoenix. It's such a generic online university. If anyone traces that university where you took classes back to prison, you're in trouble."

"Who's going to check, Princess? All that gal wanted was her interview. She's not exactly a reporter."

Laura frowned. She knew he was probably right, but she was still mad.

Axel drew his hand over his bald head and paced in his office.

"Louse problem in prison?"

"What?"

"You're bald."

"So?"

"I figured you shaved your head because of a louse problem in prison."

"Lice, fleas, assholes," he replied.

"Oh, do you swing that way?" Laura asked, flipping her wrist. "You'll love Midtown then."

"I'm not gay, Princess," he said through gritted teeth.

"Whatever."

Laura then looked carefully around her. "Hey, are you living in this office?"

"What?"

"Are you living in this office?"

"Why do you ask?"

"Hot plate, mini fridge, and that deflated air mattress in the corner."

Axel sighed. "Yes, I'm living here. It's just temporary."

"*You* are just temporary, Axel. Jesus. Does Kyle know?"

"He knows. I had to tell him. But I told him it's only temporary."

"Is it only temporary?

"Of course, it is."

"What if your parole officer finds out?"

"He knows I'm living here, too. I had to put it on my paperwork. I can't lie about it. That's a violation of my parole. And I sure as shit don't want to go back to prison."

"Oh."

"Hey, don't judge me, Princess. It's not like I got out of prison with wads of cash and could live in a fancy penthouse like you."

"Fuck you, Axel."

Just then Laura's cellphone pinged. It was time to head back to the interview with the deejay.

"Showtime, Axel. Don't fuck it up this time."

Laura walked through her front door and pulled off her boots right after she sat down. She hadn't felt good about the day. Axel was a disaster. He couldn't remember his script and she hoped the media didn't check that university he'd talked about on the radio.

She was glad she and Craig were going out that night. She needed to just not think about Axel and her work.

"We are going up to Avalon? Really?"

"Yes," Craig said as Laura strapped on her seatbelt. "I want to drive this baby." He wrapped his fingers around the steering wheel.

Laura knew Craig was very proud of his Porsche 911 Carrera and she knew he liked to drive it fast. And she knew he'd drive it fast up Georgia 400.

Laura did enjoy her meal at Oak Steakhouse in Avalon. She ordered the filet mignon, but she and Craig ordered some scallops as starters. The pair also ordered the Brussel sprouts and cauliflower as their shared sides.

Laura couldn't finish her steak, so she asked for a box. She wasn't letting a good steak go to a waiter's dog. She'd have it for lunch tomorrow.

When they'd finished their meal, without dessert, they waited at the valet station for Craig's car. The valet stepped out of the Porsche while another valet opened the passenger door for Laura.

Craig roared out of the parking lot and in a couple of turns was headed south on Georgia 400. She knew drivers sometimes sped fast on the road. It was fairly straight and three lanes.

Craig was no exception when it came to speeding. He opened up the Porsche and was driving well over 100 miles an hour, weaving in and out of traffic.

Laura was massaging Craig's crotch when blue lights appeared behind them.

"Oh shit! Laura, stop that!"

Laura jumped when she heard the police siren, putting her hand back in her lap.

Craig pulled over on the shoulder, the blue strobe lights creating eerie shadows on the dashboard.

"Shit, shit, shit," Craig said as the police officer approached the driver's window. Craig lowered the window.

"License, insurance and registration, sir," the officer said.

Craig pulled his driver's license and insurance card from his wallet, then dug through the glove box for his registration.

He found it and handed it through the window.

"Do you know how fast you were traveling, Mr. Dawson?"

"It was a little over the speed limit, I admit."

"If by a little you mean a lot, then yes. I clocked you at 101 miles per hour."

"Oh," was all Craig could say. "Sorry."

The police officer went back to his patrol vehicle and Craig began swearing under his breath. Laura was unhappy too.

"You had to show off in this car."

"Shut up, Laura. That's not helping me."

"Well, you'll get a ticket and that will be that."

"Except I have a couple of tickets already for speeding."

"Craig!"

"I know, I know. But I like to drive this car fast. What's the use of getting a car like this and going the speed limit?"

The police officer seemed to be taking a while back in his vehicle and Craig got more and more nervous. "What's taking him so long?"

The officer got out of his patrol car and approached Craig's driver's window.

"Mr. Dawson, I'm charging you with speeding and with being a super speeder since you were in excess of 100 miles per hour. I am also suspending your driver's license since you have several other speeding tickets. Please step out of the vehicle."

"Am I being arrested?"

"No, but I need you to sign these traffic citations."

"And then we can go home?"

"You cannot drive. You are lucky you have an adult passenger. Otherwise, I would have had to impound your car."

Laura could hear the conversation and began to seethe inwardly. Why did Craig have to show off in the car? she wondered. Now he'd be in a bad mood, and he wouldn't be able to perform tonight.

"Laura," Craig said, his voice tight, "could you step out of the car, please?"

Laura stepped out of the Porsche and walked over to Craig and the officer.

"You are going to have to drive me home," Craig said.

"Home? Aren't we going back to my place?"

"I need you to drive me home, please. The officer has suspended my license and I can't drive it back to my house."

"Then how am I going to get home?"

"I'll call you an Uber."

"You expect me to stand outside your house waiting for an Uber where your wife can see me?"

The officer looked up at that statement.

"Please, Laura. Drive me home. We can discuss this further in the car."

The officer handed several sheets of paper to Craig, who now looked pale and ill.

"Fine. Give me your keys."

Craig handed the keys to Laura.

"Ma'am, please drive safely and at the speed limit."

"You can bet I will," Laura said, glaring at Craig.

Craig got in the passenger's side while Laura got behind the wheel. She pulled the seat way up and moved the mirrors so she could see. The blue lights still strobed behind her.

She carefully pulled back out on the road, the officer pulling out behind her to make sure she was safely on the road and drove slightly under the speed limit to Craig's house. The couple was silent for the entire uncomfortable ride.

Chapter 3

The first month Axel's Motors was open, business was slow. Axel often had to send techs home because there was no work for them. He paid them, but he knew this wasn't the way to run a business.

Kyle had several conference calls with Axel about keeping the books and making quarterly projections, as he expected from managers of all of his investments.

By the first week of April, however, a steady stream of customers came through the business. Oil changes were the bread and butter of Axel's Motors, but Axel had a few cars and trucks to repair as well.

He didn't have to send a single tech home early that week. Axel always asked his customers how they heard about Axel's Motors. A few said they saw it when they drove by, and others heard the radio broadcast and decided to give him a chance.

Laura had stopped by the shop at least once a week. Otherwise, she was working from home on the publicity she did for Star 1 winery in Napa Valley, Buon Cibo restaurant in Buckhead and a few other freelance projects Kyle didn't know about. Star 1 and Buon Cibo were also two of Kyle's investments.

She worked on getting Buon Cibo a table at the Atlanta Food & Wine Festival, which was coming up the first weekend in June. Even though her relationship with chef/owner Simon Beck had ended badly, they were at least civil to each other now.

Her relationship with Bobby Pearce, the manager of the winery, never recovered. They sent emails to each other, but never spoke over the phone. She was still angry with him for kicking her out of his hotel when he'd been in Atlanta last fall.

Her current relationship with Craig was on thin ice. After she'd had to drive him home in his Porsche, she had indeed waited outside and down the street from his house for an Uber.

She hadn't worn a warm coat since she hadn't expected to be waiting outside in the cool March air.

Craig apologized profusely and sent her flowers the next day. Still, Laura was grateful she could work from home since she had a sore throat.

With Craig unable to drive, they couldn't go out to dinner or have sex at her place unless he took an Uber to her condo, and so far, he hadn't even mentioned it. She knew he was trying to get his suspended license back, but she imagined he was having to Uber into work and to client meetings.

Laura snorted her derision at the thought. Serves him right, she huffed. She got up and fixed a cup of tea, putting some honey in it to soothe her throat, which was bothering her.

Laura realized she was going to have to stop by Axel's Motors later in the week. She planned to meet some more car enthusiasts there. Each had a modest social media presence and she hoped they would generate a little more business for the shop, especially if she decided to do a weekend event at the shop where the enthusiasts brought their cars.

She had tried to pitch some media stories at community newspapers, but after the initial opening and subsequent stories, she was having a hard time getting anything else placed. She did a couple of advertorial stories, but she didn't want to pay for publicity. Laura wanted it for free.

Shortly after she finished eating her lunch, Craig called her on her cell.

"Hello, Craig. Haven't heard from you in a while."

"Sorry about that, Laura. I've been trying to get my driver's license back and working on several big industrial deals."

"How are you getting to work?"

"I've worked from home several days and my wife is driving me a couple of times a week."

"I'm sure she loves that. How did you explain to your wife how you got home that night?"

"I told her one of my co-workers drove me home. Remember, I was supposed to be out on a business dinner."

"And she believed you?"

"I'm sure she didn't since no co-worker stayed in the house for the Uber ride. And no car pulled into the driveway to drop me off. But she hasn't said anything."

"So why are you calling?"

"I wanted to thank you again for driving me home. And I wanted to see if you want to go to Amelia Island with me when my deal closes."

"You mean, you need a ride."

"Well, yes, but when this deal closes, I have a commercial real estate conference in Florida. I'd like to attend it and I'd like to attend it with you."

"Not your wife?"

"Not my wife."

"How will you explain your absence?"

"I'll say it's a work thing. A conference of all real estate guys, which is true. She hates that. She says it's boring. Plus, she's got some tennis tournament going on that weekend anyway."

"Where are we staying?"

"The Ritz-Carlton."

"Oh, I like that."

"I thought you would."

"And won't your coworkers wonder why you aren't there with your wife?"

"The guys who will be there aren't from my firm. They don't know my wife and, surprise, it will be you."

"When are we going?"

"Last weekend in April. The weather should be nice in Florida."

"I hope so. And when you are in your boring meetings, I'll be on the beach. There is a beach there, right?"

"There is a beach, a pool, and servers if you want drinks or food."

"I can hardly wait."

"You did me a solid after those speeding tickets. I want to return the favor."

Laura hung up with Craig and began Googling the resort and what was nearby. This was the kind of thanks she had expected when the flowers first arrived. She was glad she kept her mouth shut when Craig called. She certainly wanted to go on this trip. She felt like she needed a little vacation, too.

Laura had been working hard for Kyle and hadn't had much time away since she went to Napa last summer. She still shuddered when she thought of how that trip ended, with her in the hospital with a broken wrist and one of the winery hands arrested for her attempted murder.

She had visited her parents twice last year in Miami. She called more regularly now, and her mother was pressuring her to come down for another visit.

Laura was relieved her father had recovered from his heart attack. But Laura wasn't quite sure she was ready for another visit. Her mother was pressuring her to start a family.

In this moment, Laura wished with all her heart that Rico hadn't died, for many reasons. But the biggest one is he could have continued the family line, taking the pressure off her.

With him gone, her mother, Carmela, wanted grandchildren. And Laura was her only hope.

Laura had a close call last year when she discovered she was pregnant. She had no intention of keeping the baby, especially since the father, Simon Beck, had gone back to his wife. She had miscarried while she was in Miami helping to nurse her father after his heart attack.

Then she learned her mother had also suffered many miscarriages. Maybe the Lucas women were cursed with infertility. Laura shook her head to clear those thoughts. She certainly didn't need to think about becoming a mother. She didn't even like children.

After her pregnancy scare and miscarriage, she came back to Atlanta and saw her doctor to get back on the pill. This time, she religiously took her birth control. She certainly didn't want to get pregnant with Craig.

When she arrived at Axel's Motors the next day, she told Axel she was going out of town for a little vacation later that month.

"Will I be able to get in touch with you?" Axel asked, somewhat alarmed. "What if something happens and I need your publicity help?"

"Axel, I'm a phone call away and I'll have my laptop. I can help you if needed. But I really hope you don't need me. I'm ready for a break. Plus, I think you'll be fine. Customers are really coming in. You'll be so busy you won't even think to call me."

"I hope you are right."

"I am right. Trust me, Axel."

"Kyle told me not to trust you, Laura."

"Well, fuck Kyle."

Axel laughed at Laura's outspokenness.

"Princess, you are one ballsy bitch to talk about your employer like that."

"Listen, it's why he wants me as an employee. I'm not one of his yes men. I'm going to tell him how it is. If he doesn't like that, too bad."

"Well, just keep your cellphone on while you are balling your boyfriend on this trip."

"How did you know I have a boyfriend?"

"You don't look like the type to have a girlfriend."

Laura narrowed her eyes. "What? I don't look like a lesbian? What do lesbians look like, Axel? You are homophobic."

"Chill out, Princess. I guessed you had a boyfriend. That's all."

"Oh. Well, I don't like to divulge my personal life. I didn't think I had told you about my boyfriend."

"Your secret is safe with me."

Laura picked Craig up at his office and they headed for Florida. With Craig's suspended license, she wouldn't even entertain the idea of his driving her Mercedes, even though he offered to help drive down on the trip.

Laura took Interstate 75 south until she got to Interstate 16 in Macon, Georgia. I-16 is a long boring strip of highway, and she was glad to get to Interstate 95 near Savannah, where she headed south.

She knew there was a different way to go, but she liked the views of the marsh and water as she headed south to Florida. Craig napped in her car while she drove. She enjoyed the silence.

They arrived late that night and checked into the resort. Laura was exhausted from driving a little more than six hours. She had only stopped for gas and to get a cup of coffee. She was ready for a glass of wine in a hot tub. She hoped Craig would join her.

They got into their room, an ocean suite with a king bed. The suite did indeed have a marble bath that would fit both her and Craig.

"Hey, babe. Let's get something to eat. I'm really hungry," he said.

"God, I'm so tired. I just want to get in that tub with a glass of wine. I see there is a bottle of champagne chilling over there," she said, pointing to a wine bucket.

"Let's get some food and then come back for the champagne. It's on ice, right? I ordered it for us. A soak in that tub will be nice after dinner. And I brought my pills. We can have a soak and have a screw tonight."

"I am a little hungry," Laura admitted. "Do you want to go to the restaurant, or order in?"

"Honestly, it will be quicker to go to the restaurant. Room service will take too long."

They walked to the seafood restaurant inside the resort and ordered some foie gras as an appetizer. Laura ordered the halibut while Craig ordered beef tenderloin.

"We're ordering surf and turf, Craig."

"I hope we are sharing."

"Of course, we are."

Craig smiled. This is why he liked Laura. She was willing to share her meal with him. His wife was not a meal sharer. They ordered a bottle of wine, a Grenache that would pair well with Craig's beef and Laura's fish.

Then they looked at the dessert menu. Usually, they skipped dessert, believing each other would be the dessert, but Laura wanted to split a ginger snap soufflé and a fruity martini. After all, she reasoned, she was only driving the elevator to their room.

Craig agreed and ordered a hot toddy as his dessert beverage. They both swayed as they made their way to the elevator. Laura began to doubt whether they would make it into the big bathtub or have sex that night.

Craig and Laura entered their suite and Craig let out a big burp.

"Well, excuse you."

"Sorry. That was a big meal. It was good though. I like that this trip is all on my company's tab. Did you see the bill for the food?"

"I did not. Do you want to open the champagne and get in the tub? We could definitely relax there."

"Babe, I'm ready for bed. After that big steak, I'm tired. Sorry."

"Do you mind if I take a soak and open the champagne? I want a nice relaxing bath. I'm still sore from the drive."

"You do whatever you want. I'm going to bed."

"Fine," Laura said, annoyed that she wasn't having sex that night.

She drew a nice hot bath and poured in some lavender bath salts that were by the tub. She then opened the champagne and poured herself a flute.

Laura stepped in and felt herself relax for the first time in a long time. She began sipping her glass, then poured herself another.

Laura found the intercom music and piped in some smooth jazz. She was just wishing she'd brought her vibrator when she heard the bathroom door open and close.

"I could hear the music and couldn't fall asleep. Want some company?" Craig asked.

"Of course."

Craig stood naked in front of her and stepped into the big tub.

"Can I pour you a glass of champagne?"

"I think I'm good. But I love seeing you naked in this tub. Your breasts are perfect orbs."

Laura moved her foot to rub Craig's crotch. "I love seeing you naked in this tub, too. Did you take your pill tonight?"

"I took it right before I got out of bed. So in about a half-hour or so."

Laura lifted her glass to Craig. "To a half hour, then."

The pair enjoyed the big tub. They soaped each other's private parts and fingered each other in the warm water. Every now and again they emptied the cool water and added more warm water to keep on with their foreplay.

By the time they dried off and went to bed it was very late, but they made love and fell asleep in each other's arms.

Craig woke up slightly hungover and unready for his real estate conference. He and Laura ordered room service for breakfast with Craig drinking several cups of coffee. He took some ibuprofen as well.

Craig headed off for his conference only slightly late and Laura put on her bathing suit and coverup and went out toward the beach.

Laura made herself comfortable in a lounge chair, giving the cabana boy Craig's room number. She was enjoying the beach life at a high-end resort.

Laura reapplied her sunscreen several times, and when she got hot and hungry, she put on her coverup and sat down for lunch at the outdoor grill. She enjoyed fresh shrimp and a glass of white wine.

Since she didn't want to be out in the sun in the afternoon, Laura booked a facial and massage at the spa for later that afternoon. She charged everything to Craig's room.

Laura returned to the hotel suite and found Craig on his cellphone.

"Where have you been? We have a cocktail party in 15 minutes," he said, putting his hand over the cellphone's microphone.

"I got a massage. I feel like a noodle. I can be ready in 15 minutes. Let me get dressed."

Craig went back to his phone call. Laura could hear him talking about real estate, so she assumed he was striking a deal, even on his vacation.

Laura pulled a royal blue wrap dress out of the hotel's closet. She put on some sapphire stud earrings and a sapphire ring. She pulled out her silver Jimmy Choo stiletto heels, which had a decorative tassel hanging from the strap.

She pulled her hair up in a messy bun and put on a modest amount of makeup. With her recent facial, she knew she had a natural glow that evening. She'd gotten a modest tan and the massage oils made her skin glow. She'd gone ahead and gotten a manicure and pedicure as well. Why not?

She came back out into the living room suite and heard Craig still on the phone, but his back was to her.

"Ahem," she said, trying to catch his attention.

Craig turned and his eyes widened. "Hey, we'll finish this up later tonight," he said to the person on the phone. He hung up and then said, "Wow. You look amazing."

"I'm ready. Are you?"

"I don't want to go if you look like this."

"Now that I'm all dressed up, we are going."

"Party pooper. Let's go then."

Craig took Laura by the arm and led her out the door. They went down to a small hospitality room where several people were already there, drinks in hand. It was an open bar. Craig and Laura went to one of the bar stations.

"What are my options for white wine?" Laura asked the barkeeper.

"Chardonnay, Sauvignon Blanc, and prosecco."

"Oh, I'll have a glass of prosecco."

"Coming right up. And for you sir?"

"I'll have a G&T."

"Is Tanqueray OK?"

"That's perfect."

Drinks in hand, Craig began working the room. Laura stood at his elbow but just made small talk. This was Craig's function and event. She just wanted the beach and spa treatments.

After about an hour, the couple and the others were seated for dinner in a private dining room. The choices were chicken, shrimp, a steak, or a vegetarian meal.

"I doubt they'll serve many of the veggie meals. Us real estate guys are meat-eaters," Craig joked with his tablemates.

Laura smiled politely but was worried that Craig was drinking his gin and tonic too fast. He'd ordered another one before they entered the room for the dinner.

The servers began to come around with a choice of red or white wine. Craig asked for red. He planned on getting a steak.

Laura asked for the white wine. She wanted the shrimp. It was so good this afternoon and tasted so fresh she wanted it again that night.

After the dinner, Craig lingered in the dining room, chatting with several attendees. Laura was standing next to him, but her feet were beginning to ache. She leaned into Craig and told him she was returning to the room.

Craig waved her off, another gin and tonic in his hand. "I'm going to stay just a little longer. I won't be too long."

"Take your pill," Laura whispered in his ear. Then she smiled at Craig and turned to find the hotel room.

An hour later, Craig finally returned to the room, drunk.

"Sorry, babe. I've got to get to bed. I've got some meetings in the morning with that guy I met tonight," he said, slurring his words.

"Fine," Laura huffed and rolled her back to him in the bed.

Chapter 4

Laura and Craig argued in the car as they left Florida. "Some vacation! You were drunk nearly every night. I hardly got any sex!" she shouted.

"Listen, don't yell. My head still hurts."

Laura started blowing the car horn, just to piss Craig off.

"Stop that!" Craig yelled. "You are acting like a child. And you can't tell me you didn't have a nice time. You ran up nearly a thousand dollars at the spa. Jesus Christ! I'll probably have to pay for that."

"I thought you said your company was paying for everything."

"Not for nearly a thousand dollars spent at the spa! What the hell did you have done?"

"Not that it is any of your business, but I had a full-body massage, a facial and had my nails done. And I had some cocktails. And I fucking deserved it!" she shouted.

Craig scowled and Laura looked straight ahead as they drove in uncomfortable silence the rest of the way back to Atlanta until they got close to Laura's condo.

"Stop at my office, then you go home."

"Your office? Are you going to drive your car home? Is your car there? What about your suspended license?"

"I'll chance it. I don't want my wife to see your car."

"You've been lying to me, Craig."

"Deal with it."

Laura got back to her condo and tossed her overnight bag on her bed. She unpacked it quickly. She'd send her clothes to the cleaners tomorrow.

The more she thought about the weekend, the more she seethed at Craig. She felt it was time to end their relationship once again.

Then she got a call from a number she didn't recognize. She didn't answer it, but the caller left a voicemail. It was Craig's wife.

"I know you were with my husband this weekend. Don't see or call him again."

That cinched it. Her relationship with Craig was officially over.

Monday morning Laura's cellphone rang early.

"What's up, Axel?"

"I need to get more security cameras installed around the shop and inside the shop."

"Why?"

"Some guy tried to break in last night."

"Sunday night?"

"Yeah."

"How do you know?"

"I was here. I'm living in the shop, remember? It woke me up."

"Was there damage? Did he break-in?"

"He broke the window to the side entrance, but he didn't get in."

"And you know it's a man?"

"I checked to see what was on the security tape, but it's grainy. It looked like a man, based on the build."

"Shit. Did you call Kyle?"

"Yeah. I called him first. Woke him up."

"OK. Let me get showered and I'll be down as soon as I can. I'll check with Kyle. If he wants me to, I'll get some quotes on better security systems."

Laura hurried to get ready and headed down to Axel's Motors. She could see some cardboard covering the side door's window when she pulled into the parking lot.

It had worried her that Axel's Motors looked better than the businesses around it.

Laura could see a couple of police cars still in the parking lot, but the officers were talking to Axel, and it seemed like they were about to leave.

Axel shook their hands and the officers left. He and Laura walked into the lobby of the service station, where Axel had some coffee brewing.

"Want a cup?"

"No thanks. I had mine this morning. I'm glad you called the police," Laura said. "What did they say?"

"Made me nervous to talk to the cops. They said what they always say. Crime is up everywhere. Get an alarm system."

"We can get a better alarm system."

"I'm the best alarm system we have. And I don't want an alarm going off at night when I'm trying to sleep."

"Don't they make silent alarm systems that go right to the alarm company?"

"I don't know."

"You shouldn't be nervous around the cops. You didn't do anything wrong."

"I had to hide my gun in the office."

Laura's eyes widened. "Your gun? Why do you have a gun?"

"I live in the shop, Princess, remember? I need it for protection."

"Protection? A big lug like you? You don't need protection. You need a brain in your head."

"This area is not all that nice when the sun goes down. I feel safer with it near me."

"You know you're not supposed to have a gun."

"Are you going to tell my parole officer?"

"Worse. I might tell your brother."

"Kyle's my stepbrother. And don't you dare, Princess."

"Or what?"

Axel grabbed Laura's right wrist and applied pressure. Laura yelped in pain then felt her gaze darken and began zoning out. She then started to scream.

"Stop it! Stop it! Julio! You're hurting me!"

Axel could see the fear on Laura's face. She'd gone pale and her eyes were wild. He'd seen that look in prison when fellow inmates were having a PTSD episode.

Laura tried to hit Axel, but he batted her left hand away and dropped her wrist. But his fingers snagged Laura's beaded onyx bracelet. The elastic of the bracelet snapped and broke. Dark black beads bounced and scattered across the concrete floor.

"Breathe, Laura, breathe," he said in a soothing tone. "You're OK. No one is hurting you."

Axel steered Laura toward the white leather couches and sat her down. "Take a deep breath in. Breathe out through your mouth like you are blowing out a candle," he commanded.

"I know how to breathe asshole. I take yoga."

But Laura did take some deep breaths, trying to calm her racing heart.

"Who's Julio?"

"You broke my bracelet!" Laura said, her eyes beginning to water. She stood up from the couch rubbing her right wrist. "Help me get these beads."

Laura got down on her hands and knees trying to scoop up the onyx beads.

"I'm sorry. I'll pay to have your bracelet fixed."

"Damn straight you will."

"So, who's Julio?" Axel asked again.

"Not that it's any of your business, but he's an old boyfriend."

"Sounds like he was more than that."

"No, just an old boyfriend."

"Who hurt you?"

Laura stood up and put her hands on her hips while Axel kept trying to scoop up beads.

"Haven't we all been hurt by love?" she said, trying to sound calm.

"No, I mean he physically hurt you."

"You're being ridiculous."

"And you are changing the subject."

Laura could see more beads and got down on the floor to retrieve them. "It's none of your business."

"Will he come around looking for you? Then it is my business."

"He won't come looking for me because he's dead."

"How'd he die?"

"My brother shot him. Then the same drug gang Julio was in killed my brother."

"I'm sorry." Axel was also on his hands and knees next to Laura, trying to reach under the couch, where a few more beads had rolled. Axel then reached for one underneath Laura and brushed against her breast.

"Hey! Watch your fucking hands, mister."

34

Axel and Laura both scrambled up off the floor.

"Sorry. Here," he said, putting a handful of beads in her hand. "You can get the rest yourself. Put them on my desk and I'll take them to a jeweler to be fixed. Or I could just buy you a new one."

"This was my mother's. You'd better fix it."

"Was? I thought you said your mother is alive."

"She is. She gave this to me as a gift."

"I'll have it fixed then."

"You better."

"Now, don't you have some security and alarm companies to call?"

"Fuck you, Axel." Laura turned on her stiletto heel, marched into his office, slammed the beads on his desk, then walked out the door. She could do all the research from the comfort of her own condo.

By the time she got home, Laura started to feel angry. Angry at Axel for hurting her; angry for the broken bracelet; and angry with Craig as well.

None of this was Craig's fault, but she thought if she'd just had sex more than once over the weekend, she wouldn't have had the reaction to Axel squeezing her wrist. She rubbed her wrist again. She no longer had the pins in it, but it still bothered her now and again, especially when some asshole like Axel squeezed it hard.

Laura got on her laptop and found the top security firms in metro Atlanta. She emailed Kyle asking if she should go ahead and get price quotes for more security at the shop.

Kyle said he agreed to her getting price quotes but told her not to commit to anything without his approval.

Laura emailed a few of the firms asking for quotes and called a few others. She ended up with quotes from six security firms. They offered a variety of systems and services, all at different prices. Laura typed up the quotes and emailed the list to Kyle.

Laura decided to quit early. She'd let two of Craig's calls go to voicemail and ignored three of his texts. She listened to the voicemails. Craig was apologetic. Maybe she'd give him another chance. She did get the real spa treatment out of the weekend.

She finally decided to return Craig's call.

"Are you still mad at me?" he asked when he picked up the phone.

"Yes. But I'll forgive you if you come over and give me a decent screw."

"Oh, babe. I can't tonight. You know my wife knew I was with you. She's pretty mad at me, so I have to go home. I had to buy her some new jewelry."

"I know she's mad at you. She called me to say never to see you again."

"She called you?" Craig asked in alarm.

"I didn't recognize the number, so I let it go to voicemail."

"Shit."

"I'd like some new jewelry, too."

"You got your expensive spa day. That's enough."

Laura pouted. Not that Craig could see her pout. "Well, I want to see you. Can't you come over before you go home?"

"Are you home now?"

"Yes. Do you have your license back?"

"Not yet, but I'm willing to chance driving over there to have make-up sex with you."

"So how are you getting to and from work?"

"It's called driving with a suspended license, Laura."

"You could have helped drive us to Florida?"

"I offered, if you remember."

"I was afraid you'd get pulled over," she said.

"Well, I'm willing to do it in Atlanta. I've got too many client meetings and I can't have my wife driving me everywhere. And all the Uber rides are adding up."

"Leave work early and come over."

"I'll see you soon."

Laura thought the day was finally improving. She felt her skin tingle and dampness in her underwear. She needed to change into some lacy black undergarments. Maybe a lace bra and a thong. Maybe she'd answer the door naked and see Craig's reaction.

Around three-thirty that afternoon, her concierge called her to say Craig was on his way up. A knock came at her front door just moments later.

Laura unlocked her security system, to find Craig with a bouquet of flowers in his hand.

"I hope these will help you be less angry with me."

Laura smiled. "Let me get these in some water. There's white wine chilling in the wine fridge. Why don't you open it? Unless you'd like some red."

"Better do white. I can't drink more than a glass. I can't have a DUI on a suspended license or I'll never get my license back."

"We could forgo the wine and just head straight to my bedroom."

"Now that's a plan," Craig said as he unbuttoned his dress shirt.

Laura headed into the bedroom and slipped off her pants and blouse. Craig was undoing his belt and lowering his pants.

"Can you give me a blow job?"

Laura turned and knelt before him, pulling down his boxers. She began stroking his shaft before putting it in her mouth.

Craig put his hand on the bed to steady himself. He started to feel weak in his knees. "Maybe I should sit down," he said.

He sat on the side of the bed and Laura stopped, then started again, sucking hard.

"Sweet Jesus! Oh, God. Laura."

"Don't cum in my mouth. I want you in me."

Craig panted. "OK. Get on the bed."

Laura got off the floor and climbed onto the bed. Craig laid down next to her and unsnapped her bra and pulled down her thong.

Craig rolled on top of her and entered her, stroking hard.

"Oh, oh, oh!" Laura said, feeling her orgasm beginning to build.

She could see Craig's eyes were squeezed shut and his face began to screw up. She could see he was sweating.

Laura closed her eyes to concentrate on her own orgasm. She squeezed her vagina tight around Craig.

Suddenly, Craig was barking out his orgasm. Laura wasn't far behind. She dug her nails into Craig's back, pulling him closer into her.

They both fell back on the bed, spent. In just a few moments, both were asleep.

When Laura awoke, darkness had fallen. She poked Craig in the ribs. "Craig, Craig. We fell asleep. It's late."

"Oh shit," he said, rolling over. "Oh shit! Fuck! Fuck! Fuck!"

Craig got up and scrambled to find his clothes.

Laura got up as well, gathering her clothes.

"What time is it?"

"It's a little after nine," she replied.

"Oh, thank God. I can tell my wife I worked late. I was afraid it was after midnight."

Craig was at Laura's front door. "Let me out."

Laura unlocked the security system. "See you soon."

"See you soon," he said, and kissed her before leaving.

Laura closed the door behind him. She placed her forehead and right hand on the door, sighing.

She couldn't keep doing this. She couldn't have a man just come over and use her. She tried not to think she was using him too.

But it wasn't enough. She would just have to never see him again. The thought depressed her. She didn't like being alone.

Chapter 5

Laura had trouble sleeping that night. She once again had nightmares of Julio. Even though she didn't believe that the broken bracelet could ward off the dreams and evil eye, she still woke up rubbing her wrist, wishing it was there.

She arose before dawn and fixed her coffee. She'd go into the shop before it opened to let Axel know she had researched the upgraded security and was waiting to hear from Kyle.

As Laura put on her makeup, she looked in her mirror and noticed the dark circles under her eyes that no amount of concealer was going to cover that morning.

She felt so tired. She felt like crying. But she wouldn't allow herself to cry. She'd cried too many tears after what Julio had done. And what good did it do her?

She'd prayed and cried and felt she'd been abandoned by God. In the end, only an abortion had saved her from the shame and life of an unwed teenage mother.

Laura threw her concealer in her makeup basket and sighed. She tied her thick black hair into a messy bun and left for Axel's Motors.

Laura knocked on the side door since she knew Axel would be inside. She could see his truck locked inside one of the bays. But no one came to the door.

She stood outside for just a moment before calling his cell.

He answered out of breath.

"Where are you? I'm at the side door."

"I'm out for a run if you must know. Then I was going to swing by the gym for some weight training and a shower."

"Then how are you getting back? Are you running back? You'll be all sweaty again."

"Come by the gym and pick me up then. In about an hour."

"An hour! I'm here now. I don't want to wait outside at this hour in this neighborhood."

"Fine. I'll run over to the gym and take a quick shower. Meet me here."

"Do you have clean clothes?"

"No. I'll just put on what I have."

"And that will be all sweaty too."

"Oh, for God's sake, Princess. I don't have to be all pretty smelling like you. Customers like mechanics that stink. A sweet-smelling one makes them nervous. Come get me. I'm at the corner of Piedmont and, ah, Morningside."

"You ran all the way down to Midtown?"

"Yes. Now come pick me up."

"I don't want my car to stink from your sweat."

"Well, I don't know what to tell you. If you want me to let you in the building, I have to be there. If you don't want to come to pick me up, I'll go ahead to the gym for a shower."

"I'll meet you at your gym. Which one is it?"

"It's the LA Fitness at Ansley."

"Oh really."

"Yes, really. And I know a lot of gay men go there. Don't worry. I'm saving myself for you, Princess."

"You are going to be waiting forever."

Laura got back in her car and drove to the LA Fitness at Ansley Mall. Thankfully, there was a Starbucks in that shopping center, and she went in to get an espresso coffee. She was still very tired and now very annoyed at Axel.

She sat in her car and could see him run across the parking lot. She didn't think he saw her car. She got out her phone and texted him to text her when he was done.

About 15 minutes later she got a text that he was outside the door. Where was she?

She beeped her horn and Axel looked up and waved. He walked to her car and got in.

"Whew. Your clothes stink. Do you even wash them?"

"I wash some things in the sink of the men's bathroom at the station. Once a week I go to the laundry mat."

"I guess you are lucky there are bathrooms there. And you have the gym to shower in. And you don't need shampoo since you don't have any hair."

They pulled into the shop and Axel got out, slamming the car door.

"Hey! Be careful with my car, asshole!"

Axel unlocked the side door and stormed into the shop. Laura was right behind him, yelling at him.

"You'd better not have damaged my door!"

"Why are you always on my back?" he asked, turning to face her, now angry with her that she was angry with him.

"You know why."

"Princess, I can't change my past," Axel said, raising his voice. "I wish I could, but I can't."

Laura pointed her finger at him. "You made some bad choices."

"Are you going to stand there, so holier than thou, and tell me you never made any bad choices in your past?"

"Yes!"

"Really, Princess?" Axel said, narrowing his eyes. "What about Julio?"

Laura felt as though she'd been slapped. Axel could tell he'd struck a nerve by the look of shock on her face.

"Don't ever say his name to me again."

"I'm sorry. That was out of line."

Suddenly Laura burst into tears.

Now it was Axel's turn to be shocked. Laura was sobbing. Axel steered her to the couch and they both sat. Axel put his arm around Laura, trying to comfort her.

"I wish I'd never met him," she cried, deep wracking sobs where she couldn't catch her breath. "I have nightmares about him." She caught her breath and went quiet. "The things he did to me," she whispered.

Axel held her tighter. "I'm so sorry, Princess. A woman like you should never be hurt by a man like that."

"He's still haunting me."

"What do you mean, haunting you?"

41

"I have bad dreams about him," she said, trying to control her breathing. "That bracelet? My mother gave it to me to ward off the evil eye."

Axel guffawed. "You don't believe that bullshit, do you? The evil eye?"

Now Laura was angry again. "All I know is it worked. When I wore it, I didn't have bad dreams about him. And you broke it! Now I'm having bad dreams again."

"Look, I'm sorry. I'll take it to the jewelers on my lunch break today."

"You haven't even taken it in to be fixed?" she shrieked.

"I said I'm sorry," Axel said, anger in his voice. "I forgot. I've got a shop to run, remember? Why did you come here so early today anyway?"

"I came to tell you I priced upgraded security systems and sent a proposal to Kyle. He'll make the decision."

"Just great. He probably won't buy anything. That guy is a tightwad, you know that?"

"He's been generous to me."

"Of course, he's generous to you, Princess. But when I needed a lawyer, did he help me out? Hell no."

"He said you pleaded guilty. Didn't go to trial."

"What else could I do? I had a public defender. Kyle wouldn't help me at all."

"Well, he's helping you now, isn't he?"

"I think he feels guilty about it. That he didn't help out."

Laura rubbed her wrist. "I know what you mean. He didn't hire me full-time until I was almost killed by an arsonist at his winery last year."

"What? What happened?"

"One of the winery hands was setting fires on the property. I caught him in the office, and he doused me with gasoline and tried to set me on fire."

"Jesus! How did you get out of there?"

"I didn't. He shoved me to the floor, tossed a lighter in the room, and locked the office door behind him."

"Oh shit!" Axel said, his eyes wide.

"I'll say. It was a miracle the lighter went out and didn't ignite the fumes. I got a broken wrist for my trouble."

"Broken wrist?"

"Yeah."

"Which one? The one I squeezed?"

"That's the one, asshole."

"Oh, I'm sorry. I didn't know that."

"There's a lot you don't know about me, and I'd like to keep it that way," she snapped. "I don't want you to ever lay a hand on me again, understand?"

Axel put his hands up defensively. "I'm not touching you ever again."

"Perfect. Now I'm headed back home," Laura said, turning for the door. She then swung back around to face Axel, giving him a fake smile. "Have a nice day."

Laura got back to her condo, turned, and locked her security system, and went straight back to bed. She felt so fatigued. Her emotional outburst had been draining – and embarrassing. She didn't like to lose control of her emotions. She didn't like disclosing her personal business, either. And she'd done both.

She awoke several hours later to two missed texts and a missed call from Kyle. She quickly got out of bed and read the messages.

Kyle said he needed her out in Napa in mid-May. Star 1 would be part of a wine and food festival and two of the winery's vintages would be up for awards. The three-day event included a winemaker's dinner.

Bobby Pearce was going to need help running the booth at the festival and would need supplementary publicity help.

Kyle wasn't asking her if she could go. He was ordering her to go.

But another free trip to Napa and maybe another chance to hook up with Bobby? Laura smiled. She quickly texted Kyle back apologizing for not responding right away and said she'd be happy to go. Would he be sending his private plane for her?

Kyle called back, rather than text her his reply.

"Laura, book a flight to San Francisco. I'll have Bobby pick you up."

"First class?"

Kyle sighed. "Yes, go first class. You'll be there May 17 through 21, so make your plans accordingly."

"That doesn't give me much time to get ready. Didn't Bobby know about this ahead of time?"

"I've already discussed it with him. No need to tear him a new one, Laura."

"OK. I'll do some research on the festival and prepare some talking points. What wines are up for awards?"

"The ones we both like. The Cabernet reserve and the merlot."

"Great. I'll work up some releases about both wines. I'll run them by Bobby to make sure what I say is what is right. Does he need a release about Star 1 being featured in the festival?"

"Wouldn't hurt but call him and work that out with him."

"Is he going to return my calls?"

"He hasn't been?"

"Not lately."

"Laura, I have a feeling there's more to this story that will only make me angry if I find out what it is."

"I'll call him. I'll tell him we have to work together to get this done."

"Fine."

Suddenly, Laura realized just how busy she was going to be for the rest of May. She was heading out to Napa for Star 1's event and had work to do ahead of Buon Cibo's being in the Atlanta Food and Wine Festival at the end of May.

She'd also likely have to oversee whatever new security system Kyle chose for Axel's Motors. She texted Kyle back to ask if he'd decided on the upgraded security system. Not yet, was his reply.

Well, at least she wouldn't have that to worry about just yet.

Chapter 6

Laura settled into her first-class seat on a Delta flight to San Francisco. Bobby Pearce had been surprisingly polite in their conversations for the past week, and he said he'd pick her up at the airport.

She sipped on a mimosa before the flight began. This was the life she wanted to lead. If she couldn't be on Kyle's private jet, she wanted to travel first class.

For lunch, she opted for the chicken salad on a warm brioche bun, a mixed green salad, and a glass of white wine.

Not one for small talk with a fellow passenger, Laura was grateful her seatmate had eyeshades on and appeared to be napping.

About an hour before landing, the flight attendant asked if Laura would like her wine topped off. She gladly accepted the refill.

She texted Bobby when she landed. He told her where to wait outside after she deplaned. Then she saw his familiar work truck rumble up to the curb. He started to get out of his truck to help with her bag, but she waved him off. She had a small carry-on and put it in the small space behind her passenger seat.

"Thanks for picking me up. Saves me from having to rent a car."

"You're welcome," he said, as he pulled out into traffic to exit the airport.

They were silent as Bobby drove, but then he said, "Listen, I just want to make one thing clear. We are not getting back together."

"I didn't expect that we were. You made yourself very clear last year."

"I'm seeing someone else now, Laura."

"That's wonderful. I'm happy for you."

Bobby looked over at Laura to see if she meant it.

"You know her."

"I do? Who are you seeing?"

"Kimberly Gifford. That reporter that interviewed me."

"Kimberly?" Laura asked, her eyes getting wide. "She's a little young, isn't she?"

Bobby's face darkened. "You know what? She's a nice person and she and I get along. Age is just a number."

"OK, Bobby. As I said, I'm glad you found someone. I'm glad you are happy."

"Why do I find it hard to believe you?"

Laura let out a big sigh. "Listen, I didn't fly across the country to argue with you. I just want the festival to go well and for Star 1 to win some awards, OK? You date or see or fuck whoever you want."

"I want the festival to go well, too. I've never done one before. I know I should have done them, but as an owner, I didn't have time. As manager I really don't have that much time, either, which is why I asked Kyle if you'd come out. I need some help."

"That's why I'm here, Bobby. To help you and do whatever publicity I can. If you need me to schedule any media, I can do that, too. I sent you the press releases about the wines. I hope I got it all correct."

"I got those. We'll go over the details when we get to the winery. There's just a couple of things we need to change."

"Do you want to go to Star 1 first and get it out of the way?" Laura asked. "Then can you drop me off at the B&B?"

"Sure."

They didn't talk again until Bobby pulled into the long driveway to the winery.

"Hard to believe I was here just last year."

"And a lot has happened since then," he said, pulling up to the office, which had been renovated since the fire. They went in and Bobby sat at his desk. There was a nice chair in there, and Laura sat down. Laura noticed it was a lot nicer than the wooden crate she'd had to sit on last year.

"What happened to Walker Folks?" she asked, referring to the man who tried to set the fire that would have killed her.

"He pled guilty. He never said who he was working for or starting the fires for. I have my suspicions."

"Who do you think he was working for?"

"Nope. Not going to say. Don't want to be accused of slander if I'm wrong."

"Is Walker in prison?"

"He's still in prison. He pled guilty to the arson and to the assault on you. He should have gotten attempted murder for what he did, but it was a lesser aggravated assault charge. He'll be in for a couple of years and then get out on parole. I'll get a restraining order so he can't come anywhere near the winery."

"I still have nightmares about him," Laura said softly. "In my dreams I still see his face when he lit that lighter."

"Jesus, I'm glad you weren't killed."

"Me, too."

Bobby let out a sigh. "I am sorry about all of that. I never wanted to see you hurt."

"Let me know when he gets out of prison. I suppose I'll need a restraining order, too. But I doubt he's coming across the country to harm me again."

"You can speak when he's up for parole. You can voice your concerns. I'll be there."

"I don't know. I don't want to talk about that now. Let's pull up those releases about the wine and fix those. I'm ready to get to my B&B and relax."

"Do you have dinner plans tonight?"

"I don't. Are you inviting me to dinner?"

"Kimberly and I are going to cook out tonight. We'd love to have you join us. The first day of the festival begins tomorrow and we'll be busy."

"I think I'll pass tonight. I'm planning to go to bed early tonight so I'm ready for tomorrow. I'm on East Coast time, remember? You know what we need? An intern. If we had one, he or she could help us at festivals like this one."

"Good idea. Are you going to ask Kyle about it?"

"Yes, when I get back. Right now, let's get these releases fixed and then drive me to my B&B."

Laura was glad she could get a room at the B&B. With the festival in the area, she had to pay extra for a larger suite. Well, Kyle was paying for it, but she knew he'd want her to stick to a budget.

This suite had a deep claw-footed tub as well and she was really looking forward to that.

She ordered from Uber Eats and had a meal delivered to the B&B. Before she left the winery, she asked Bobby if she could have a couple of bottles of wine. He went to the storage area and pulled out two bottles of the Cabernet reserve that was up for an award.

Her room came with a complimentary bottle of wine as well and a cheese plate with some chocolate-covered strawberries. But she just used the wine opener on the better wine.

Laura had ordered a small salad and a pork tenderloin with potatoes. She'd tried to pair her food with the full-bodied wine she had opened.

She drew a hot bath and put in some of the B&B's complimentary lavender bath salts. She took a relaxing soak, and then went to bed. She was tired and she knew it would be a busy three days of the festival.

Laura awoke groggy, a little hungover from all the wine she'd had. She had set her alarm for seven in the morning, but it felt like it was earlier than that. She rolled out of bed and immediately started the coffee maker in her suite.

She dressed and went down for breakfast before she texted Bobby to see if he was up and ready for her to come to the festival site to help set up.

Bobby said he'd meet her there. She ordered an Uber and arrived just before Bobby's truck pulled up.

"It's going to be a long day," Bobby said. "We have a table, number 35. As soon as we find it, I'll start bringing the cases of wine over."

"Can we leave the wine here? Will they secure the festival? Or will we need to bring the wine back to your truck this evening?"

"They told me they will secure the festival. And you and I will then go to the dinner."

"You aren't taking your girlfriend?"

"She has to work tonight."

"Well, I won't turn down a good meal and good wine."

She and Bobby worked side by side all day, greeting festivalgoers, talking about the wines, talking about the winery. Laura had her iPad running the website's video footage and occasionally signed up someone to the winery's newsletter.

"Good thinking on the iPad. I wouldn't have thought to do that," Bobby said, during a lull in the crowds.

"That's why I'm your publicist."

At five o'clock that afternoon, the festival closed for the day. Laura sat down on the chair beside their table. She pulled off her boots and rubbed her feet.

"I noticed you wore your boots. Glad you didn't wear those awful sandals you like."

"Ha! I knew I'd be on my feet all day. But my feet still ache."

"We have about two hours before the dinner tonight. Do you want me to drive you back to your B&B?"

"That would be wonderful. I'll take an Uber back here, but I'd like to freshen up and change clothes."

"I can drive you home tonight, so don't worry about getting an Uber after dinner."

"Thanks. I appreciate it."

Laura wanted to lay down on the bed and grab a power nap, but she knew she couldn't. She changed clothes, had another cup of coffee, and ordered an Uber. She arrived back at the festival a little after seven o'clock.

Winery managers and owners were milling around the cocktail event space. Dinner would be inside the banquet hall.

Laura found Bobby talking with another winery owner. She was reintroduced to Sean King. She remembered him from last year. Bobby had said Sean had expressed an interest in purchasing Star 1 when Bobby was nearing bankruptcy, but Kyle had come in as an investor and saved the winery from financial ruin.

The trio chatted for a moment before Bobby saw another vintner and steered Laura to make introductions.

They all had glasses of wine, mostly reds. A few of the guests had some white wine.

"Hey, I wanted to ask you," Laura said when she and Bobby had a moment alone. "My Uber driver was talking about wildfires in the area. Are they close?"

"Not to Star 1," Bobby replied. "But it is concerning. We have wildfires in California a lot, unfortunately. But the smoke from the fires can ruin the grapes. I'm keeping an eye on where the fires are. Don't worry."

Laura frowned. "If you are sure the winery isn't in danger."

"It's not. I'd let Kyle – and you – know."

Eventually, the guests were called into the banquet hall for dinner. It was catered by Celadon, one of the restaurants she'd eaten at last year with her former client and lover Marc Linder.

Appetizers included a choice of a roasted beet salad or an arugula salad. Entrees were a choice of filet mignon, roasted chicken, or salmon. Various sides included sautéed spinach and truffle fries.

Laura and Bobby both chose the filet mignon and paired it with a cabernet from a nearby winery. Bobby joked he needed to drink the wines of the competition.

A variety of pastries were served for dessert. Laura turned hers down. She was full and getting very sleepy. Bobby had two bites of a lava cake, then said he was ready to go.

"Are you ready?" he asked Laura.

"I am."

Bobby dropped off Laura before driving back to Star 1. He smiled in the dark at how pleasant the evening had been. Why couldn't Laura behave this way all the time? They might still be together if…, he thought.

Bobby shook his head to clear his mind. Stop thinking about the what ifs, he told himself as he drove.

Laura stripped naked and fell into bed. Her head hurt from having to be so nice to Bobby when she really just wanted to take his clothes off and make love to him.

Laura and Bobby spent the second day of the festival much like the first. Talking to crowds of people, pouring wine, and inviting groups to take a tour of the winery. Laura also made sure she pointed out the winery was available for bridal showers, baby showers, and weddings. She got more people to sign up for the newsletter.

By the end of the second day of the festival, Laura was in the chair rubbing her aching feet again.

"When is the awards ceremony?"

"Tomorrow at noon," Bobby said. "It will happen during the festival. If we win, I hope everyone rushes over to buy the rest of our bottles. I don't want to have to carry them all back to the truck."

"Do we know who the competition is?"

"Basically, all the vintners here."

"Well, that narrows it down," she said, sarcastically.

"I was hoping when the judges came around earlier, they would have given us some kind of hint."

"The judges? I don't remember the judges coming around."

"Oh, you weren't at the table."

"Seriously? They came when I went to the bathroom?"

"Sorry. I couldn't exactly leave the booth to come find you. And I sure as hell wasn't going to enter the ladies' room to get you."

Laura blew out her breath. "I guess not. But it was bad timing. I wanted to be here when the judges came by."

"Well, fingers crossed our wines win something. I've heard Sean King's winery is up for an award too. I sure hope he doesn't win."

"You don't like him much, do you?"

"Can you ever like a rival vintner?"

Laura laughed. "I guess not."

The awards ceremony began later than expected as crowds had swelled for the final day of the festival. The weather had been perfect. Laura stayed at the booth, while Bobby went to the area where the winners were to be announced.

Laura could barely stand not being there. Bobby said he would text her as the awards were announced, but he texted one award, then didn't text again. She hoped that meant good news; that he was so busy going up and getting the award for Star 1, he didn't have time to text her.

In her mind, Laura began writing a release to send out to all media about the award.

Laura looked up to see Bobby walking back to the booth, surrounded by several people.

"Bobby! Did we win?"

"We got the silver," he said, looking angry.

"Silver?"

"Goddamn it, Sean King took gold," he whispered.

"Oh no. But silver is good right?"

"It's not gold."

But several festivalgoers began to crowd around Star 1's booth and bought whatever bottles and cases were left. That made Bobby smile. Laura smiled, too. She was glad she decided to stay and extra day and leave later May 22. She was going to be busy Monday posting on social media and writing press releases about the silver award.

Laura took an Uber to get to the winery early and met Bobby at the office. Bobby spent the day on the phone doing interviews and one stand-up interview with a San Francisco TV station. Laura stood by him when the TV interviews happened.

Laura spent most of the day on the phone, too, talking to the media, and sending out social media posts to Facebook, Instagram, Twitter, and Pinterest. She was thankful she had taken some photos of the Cabernet that won the award with the silver medal. She sent that photo out to all the sites.

The winery received a certificate, too, which Laura wanted professionally framed. Bobby told her to just go to a hobby store and buy a frame that would fit it. It was their first argument since she'd arrived. In the end, he said he would drop it off to be professionally framed.

Then Bobby was driving her south toward San Francisco's airport Monday evening. He dropped her off curbside at the departure area. He did come around to give her a hug. Laura might have held on longer than necessary.

Chapter 7

Laura landed in Atlanta early Tuesday morning, May 23. She got her car out of long-term parking and headed up Interstate 85 until she got off on Georgia 400's exit 2 and into Buckhead. Traffic was light that night and since she'd had a nice first-class evening meal, she didn't stop for food.

Laura, exhausted from the trip, still texted Bobby to tell him she had arrived home safely and to remind him to drop the award certificate at the frame shop the next day.

She puttered around her condo, then went to bed. She knew she'd still be on California time and hoped she wouldn't wake up too early later that morning.

Laura needn't have worried. She had nightmares about Julio and was up at four, just two hours after she'd gone to bed.

She was glad she had put a couple of wine bottles in her luggage, which she'd had to check. She opened one of the award-winning Cabernet wines and sipped it on her couch, looking out onto the balcony into the foggy street lights below.

When she felt the tension ease from her mind, she rinsed out her wineglass and went back to bed. She slept dreamlessly until she awoke at eight that morning.

Laura dragged herself out of her bed and went to the kitchen to start her cafetera coffee maker. She needed her Cuban coffee to be extra strong this morning. She whipped the coffee into a slight foam and added sugar and cream.

She sipped it slowly. She didn't have any croissants but did have a mango that was overly ripe but tasted good for her breakfast.

Laura began work that morning on the Atlanta Food and Wine Festival for Buon Cibo. The festival began May 31 and would end June 3. She had Simon Beck, the head chef — and her former lover — doing a panel discussion about Italian cuisine and doing a food demo during the event.

Buon Cibo, or "good food" in Italian, would also have a table at the festival. Sous chefs would be offering Italian appetizers and limoncello samples.

But there was a lot to do ahead of the event. Laura sent out press releases and then sent out emails to all of the staff involved to make sure it would go smoothly.

She knew she would have to be on hand and attend that festival as well.

And amid her busy day, Axel texted asking when he would get his new security system. In all of her work for other clients, she'd forgotten about the security at the service station.

She quickly texted Kyle asking if he'd decided about the security upgrade. She then texted Axel to say she was checking with Kyle.

After two hours, Kyle said he didn't want to invest any more in security. Laura frowned. That wasn't good news, considering there was already a near break-in. With reservations about Kyle's decision, she texted Axel the news.

Told you so, was Axel's response. I told you he wouldn't do it. He's a tightwad.

Sorry. You were right.

When are you coming to the shop?

Tomorrow, probably. Still jet lagged from California. And I've got work to do for Buon Cibo restaurant. Big festival in Atlanta coming up.

OK. See you tomorrow.

Laura thought it was odd that Axel wanted to see her at the shop. She could very well work from home on his publicity, which at the moment, was minimal. But she needed to keep this client happy as well, even if she wasn't happy about his past.

That same day, Simon responded to Laura's email, unhappy with his cooking demonstration.

Why am I having to do this? This should be done by a sous chef, he emailed.

Simon, I'm trying to boost you into a celebrity chef in Atlanta. It would help if you did this event. And try to be charming about it, she responded.

That comment would likely piss Simon off, but she didn't care. She was attempting to elevate his chef status. Other chefs were doing similar things at the festival. Why shouldn't he?

Meet me at the restaurant tomorrow. I want to talk to you, Simon demanded.

Laura rolled her eyes. Typical Simon, she thought. Such a prima donna.

Now she was going to have to meet Axel at his shop and Simon at his restaurant.

I'll meet you tomorrow afternoon. I have another appointment with another client in the morning, she responded.

Very well. But try to be here before four, Simon answered.

What an asshole! Laura thought. Between Axel and Simon, Laura couldn't determine which client she disliked more now.

Laura had another fitful night of sleep. She was still experiencing jet lag and she still had bad dreams. This time, she dreamt about Walker Folks, the arsonist who tried to kill her. "Die, bitch," she could hear him say before she awoke with a start.

Once again, she got up and had a glass of Star 1's Cabernet. She expected she'd need to order more wine or ask Simon if she could buy some from his restaurant. She'd get a better deal if Simon could buy it wholesale from his distributor and she could buy some from him.

This morning, she watched the sunrise from her balcony. The late-May morning in Atlanta had a slight breeze and not much humidity. She knew it wouldn't last. Before long, she'd be running her air conditioner full blast and wiping the condensation from her full-length windows.

Laura went into the kitchen to make her coffee, then showered, dressed, and headed out for her day.

She stopped first at Axel's Motors, arriving before the shop opened. She texted Axel and was grateful he was there and not out for a run or at the gym for a shower or whatever else he did when he was alone at the shop in the morning.

Axel unlocked the side door and let Laura in.

"I told you he wouldn't upgrade the security," he said bitterly. "He's leaving me out to dry."

"Well, he's got to protect his investment. But he also needs to protect you."

"Ha! You seem to think he gives a shit about me."

"Well, doesn't he? I mean he paid for this shop and set you up in it."

"I told you I think he feels guilty. It's not that he cares. He feels guilty."

"Guilty for what? Not hiring an attorney for you?"

Axel rubbed his hand on his bald head. "His father had an affair with my mother. We have the same father, but his father never married my mother. He was still married at the time. Still is. Almost led to the breakup of Kyle's parents' marriage. I was the unhappy surprise of their affair."

Axel paced around the lobby. "I'm younger. But my mother didn't want me. She didn't want a child. I ended up being raised by my grandmother."

"And you think he holds that against you? But you aren't to blame."

"Kyle was old enough to remember what happened with his folks. His father knew about me. I spent some time with him and Kyle. But I went to live permanently with my grandmother."

"Jesus. That sounds messed up."

"It was – is."

"Is that why you got into drugs?"

"I got into drugs because I was stupid and needed money."

"Sounds familiar. That's why my brother said he did it, too."

"But I wasn't stupid enough to use them."

"That's what my brother said, too, but he still ended up dead."

"I'm not going to end up dead, Princess," Axel spat.

"Well, what are you going to do about security?"

"Sleep with my gun nearby."

"Axel, that's not a good plan. What if your parole officer comes by and finds you with it?"

"He won't."

"What if you accidentally shoot someone? How will you explain that?"

"Princess, I'm not giving up my gun while I'm living in the shop. Not happening. End of story."

"Well, can we ask the police to do more patrols around the shop?"

"I'm not all that wild about the police coming around the shop when I am in possession of an illegal weapon."

"I don't know what to tell you. I wish I didn't know about the gun."

"Hey, I have your bracelet," he said, changing the subject.

Axel went back to his office and returned with a jewelry box that had the repaired bracelet. Laura lifted the box's lid.

"This isn't how it was."

"I know. It's now strung with wire, which is stronger than that old elastic you had. And I asked them to put a clasp on it. Here, let me put it on you."

Axel unhooked the clasp and placed it on Laura's right wrist, fumbling just a bit with the small clasp.

"Thank you. It feels good to have it back."

"Sweet dreams, Princess."

"I know you don't believe that the bracelet helps."

"No, no. If you think it wards off the dreams, then I'm sure it does. Some therapy might do the same thing."

"I'm not crazy, Axel," Laura said angrily.

"Says you."

"I'm leaving."

Laura walked out of the shop in a huff.

"You are a crazy bitch, Princess," Axel said under his breath as she left. "Beautiful, but crazy."

Laura enjoyed a leisurely lunch with a glass of wine at Buckhead Diner before she drove north toward Buckhead to Buon Cibo. The traffic on Peachtree Road was heavier than usual. Was there a wreck? she wondered.

She finally pulled into Buon Cibo's parking lot shortly before two and saw Simon's car there. She pulled in next to his.

Laura walked through the front door and up to the bar. She looked around. The lunch crowd was thinning, but the restaurant still had customers.

"Where is Simon? In his office?" she asked the bartender, who was wiping off a glass.

"Yeah, I'll let him know you are here."

"I know where his office is."

"No, he asked you to wait out here. I'll go get him."

Laura frowned. Why couldn't she just go to his office? They were going to be working there anyway.

Simon appeared just minutes later. "Thank you for coming today, Laura."

"Simon, can we go back to your office? We can work there."

"I'd rather we work out here."

Laura raised an eyebrow. Ah, she thought. He doesn't want us to be seen in an intimate space. His wife must have him on a short leash these days.

"Very well. Do you want to sit at that table, and I'll sit at this one?" Laura couldn't help but be snide about the arrangement.

"We can sit at the bar."

The bar. Even though it was noisy. Laura tried not to roll her eyes at Simon.

Laura frowned her displeasure as she put her laptop bag on top of the bar, pulled out her laptop and booted up her computer.

"Has the Wi-Fi password changed?"

"No," he said. "It's still the same."

"Great. Here are the press releases I've worked up for the food and wine festival, and here are press releases about the wines we're featuring. Star 1 just won a silver award, so I've put that in this one," she said, moving her computer to face him.

"Could you please print these out?"

"Sure. Same printer?"

"Same printer."

Laura hit print. "And here's a schedule of events for the festival and where you and your staff need to be during all of the days."

"Could you print those out too?"

"Sure."

"Samuel!" Simon shouted back into the kitchen. "Could you bring me the stuff off the printer?"

A dark-haired man with tattoos up his arms came over to the bar with several sheets of paper in his hands.

"You want a Coke or something?" he asked Laura.

She really wanted another glass of wine after the day she was having, but since he wasn't offering that, she replied, "Sure. Diet Coke, please."

Samuel pulled a glass from a rack, filled it with ice, and pressed the soft drink button for Diet Coke. He got a cocktail napkin from the bar service and put the glass down on it, pushing it toward Laura.

"Thanks," she said, smiling at him.

"Sorry, I should have offered you something to drink," Simon said, apologizing.

"I have it now, so don't worry."

Simon put on his reading glasses and began to look over the press releases and then the schedule for the festival. "These are three full days, Laura."

"Simon, you know it is one of the biggest food festivals in Atlanta. We need to be present, especially since Buon Cibo is one of the newer restaurants in Atlanta now."

"You've got me at a demonstration table. But you don't suggest what I should fix."

"Simon, you are the chef. You should fix whatever you feel comfortable making in a short time. You'll only have about 30 minutes or so to make the dish. That's what the organizer told me. You'll likely have to have everything pretty much prepared. You can just heat it up. But you'll need to make the dish in front of the guests. The whole demonstration will be over in an hour."

"I'll have to think about what I'll make."

"When you decide, let me know because I have to let the organizer know what you are making. And then we need to make sure we have all of the ingredients to feed about 50 ticketed guests."

"Fifty people?" he asked, looking tense.

"This demonstration table is a ticketed event. There are only 50 people allowed in. I guess we should make sure we have ingredients for 60 people, just to be safe."

"How am I going to make food for 50 people, Laura?" he asked, now visibly anxious.

"Your sous chefs will be making the food, or heating it up, behind you. You'll be front and center at the demonstration table. Everyone else will be behind you."

Laura could see Simon relax. "Thank God."

"Simon, I'll be there all weekend and I can help with any interviews you have from the TV stations or the newspapers."

"You'll be there?"

"Of course. Kyle has asked me to be there for the whole thing."

Simon gave a small smile. "Thanks. I appreciate the help."

"If you need me, you know where to reach me," Laura said, packing up her laptop.

Simon walked Laura to the front door.

"Listen, I still owe you some money for the, you know."

"No, you don't. It's taken care of."

"But you…"

"I said it's taken care of," Laura snapped. "As you once told me, you don't owe me a dime."

Laura walked out the door and didn't see the pained look on Simon's face. She would never tell him she had miscarried their baby. She'd let him think she'd had an abortion and feel guilty about not helping her pay for it.

Chapter 8

Simon decided he would make the eggplant rolls, an Italian appetizer he served at the restaurant, for his demonstration. Most of these he could prep well ahead of the table demonstration and his sous chefs could have the appetizers cooking in the portable oven while he was building it for show.

Laura let the festival organizer know what Simon would be preparing at the event, then had pre-printed recipes to hand out at the demonstration. She worked up another press release for the media.

Laura worked tirelessly in the days before the food and wine festival. Laura arrived Wednesday when the booths for the festival were being set up. She argued that Buon Cibo's booth should be closer to one of the entrances, where it would get more visibility and traffic.

She got her way. Buon Cibo's booth assignment was moved. She arrived early Thursday before the festival started. She walked off some nervous energy in the boots she had bought in Napa Valley the year before. There was no way she was wearing her high heels for this event. She'd change into her heels for the after-parties at the event.

The weekend called for rain, but she hoped it wouldn't ruin the event. She needn't have worried. The event was as crowded as she'd expected.

The Midtown Atlanta festival featured over 150 chefs, sommeliers, mixologists, and pitmasters that year. There were food and technique demonstrations, such as the one Simon was doing, and tasting tents. Laura was looking forward to the dinner events.

She felt like she walked every inch of the festival streets, which were closed to traffic. Crowds wandered with drinks and small plates at every turn.

Laura kept tabs on the Buon Cibo tent and table but also checked in on the other Seventh Heaven group restaurants. She also checked on the competition.

Some of the other vendors and restaurants at the event were 4Rivers Smokehouse, Arches Brewing, Eventide Brewing, Grand Champion BBQ, Hattie B's, New Realm Brewing, High Road Craft Ice Cream, Honeysuckle Gelato, Scofflaw Brewing, Orpheus Brewing, Second Self Beer Company, Oysters XO, Peachdish, Restaurant365, Revolution Doughnuts, and Sweetwater Brewing Company.

Friday would be a bigger crowd and more events, although forecasted rain that afternoon might chase festivalgoers away. Saturday would be the biggest day, with Sunday also busy.

On Saturday, Laura was shoulder to shoulder with crowds of festivalgoers. She had to shove her way to Simon's demonstration table, which was packed with ticket holders. Laura smiled at the crowds but could see Simon pacing behind the table. Was something wrong?

Laura hustled over to the table. "What's wrong?"

"I'm missing the olive oil! I can't sauté the eggplant for the demonstration!"

"Are you fucking kidding me?"

Laura mentally tried to think if she could rush to the store and buy some olive oil, but there wasn't time. The demonstration was just minutes from starting.

"What are we going to do?" Simon asked. "Do we cancel?"

"Absolutely not. We are not canceling. Will the dish work if you bake it or grill it?"

"I guess we'll have to grill it. I hope it turns out."

Laura felt ill. This was a disaster. How could they forget the olive oil?

A sous chef held up one small bottle of olive oil he'd found in the truck and put it on the table by Simon.

"Oh, thank God! We'll have to make do. Chefs! Use this sparingly!" he said, holding up the bottle. He poured just enough oil into his pan and handed the bottle back to his staff.

They were just heating up the already prepared eggplant. They likely wouldn't need to use any of the remaining oil.

Simon smiled at the crowd and talked amicably about how to make the dish. He chatted about the history of the dish and offered the first few plates as they came out of the oven behind him.

Laura could hear the murmurs of guests who were enjoying the appetizers. Only then could she breathe a sigh of relief.

Laura and Simon went to one of the dinner events Saturday night, and Laura got home very late.

Sunday's weather was perfect for the festival, although it was hot. Laura was glad when the festival was finally over.

She was ready for a glass of wine as Buon Cibo was closing its booth. The sous chefs poured cups of leftover wine to several of those helping to pack up. Laura had her cup refilled several times. She wasn't letting Star 1's Cabernet go to waste.

With the festival finally over, she told Kyle she needed a couple of days off. He didn't complain. She'd worked all through the weekend.

She relaxed in her condo Monday and Tuesday. She had liberated two bottles of the Cabernet as she left the festival, so enjoyed it on her penthouse's balcony watching the sunset. June was starting to get warm and humid, so she didn't stay out too long on the balcony, but there was a nice breeze both nights.

Laura was able to sleep well at night, too. No nightmares. She always kept her bracelet on only taking it off when she showered in the morning.

On Monday afternoon, Laura's condo concierge called her to let her know some flowers had been delivered for her. Laura was surprised. After her final breakup with Craig — and it was final, she swore to herself — she didn't know who would be sending her flowers.

A condo staff member brought them up to her condo. The flowers were from Simon, thanking her for her help with the festival.

Laura smiled. The arrangement was quite large, and it was a nice gesture. She also thought

there was still a little guilt involved with Simon sending her flowers. She noticed there wasn't any cash in the note thanking her for her help. Bastard, she thought, but she smiled even wider.

Laura slept in on her days off, went down to her condo's gym to work out, shopped for some food for her refrigerator, and did a yoga class she had on her DVR.

She felt refreshed Wednesday morning and ready to start the day. Now she felt ready to do some work for Axel's Motors and Star 1.

Laura texted Axel to ask if he had talked to Kyle about the security.

No. he responded. **I thought you were going to do it.**

OK. I'll reach out to him again.

Laura emailed Kyle to ask if he had reconsidered upgrading the security at Axel's Motors.

Kyle asked if there had been another break-in.

No, not since the first one, she emailed back.

I think we'll be fine with the security we have.

Laura was so tempted to tell Kyle that the "security we have" was Axel living in the shop with a gun. But that would be betraying Axel's trust and she wasn't willing to do that. As much as she didn't like him, she wasn't willing to throw him under the bus to his stepbrother.

OK, she emailed back. But I wish you would reconsider.

I'll think about it.

Laura knew what that meant. Kyle was not going to think about it and was not going to upgrade the security.

Laura decided she'd better call Axel with the news, but she got his voicemail. He must be busy at the shop. She left a voicemail asking him to call her when he got a chance.

Axel finally called her around six, shortly after the shop closed.

"Sorry. It was busy today. And I'm completely booked with work tomorrow as well."

"That's good news, right?"

"It's great news."

"I just wanted to tell you I talked with Kyle and he's not going to upgrade the security."

"I could have told you that. But thanks for trying again."

"Well, I'm sorry."

"Make it up to me," Axel said.

"What?"

"Have dinner with me tonight."

"Dinner?"

"Yeah, you know, eating, food. You do eat, don't you?"

"Of course, I do. How do you know I don't have plans tonight?"

"Do you have plans tonight?"

"No."

"Then it's settled. We'll have dinner. I hate eating alone."

"I hate eating alone too. It's amazing how many times I have to do just that," she said, suddenly realizing she was being too personal. "Are you paying?"

"Sure, Princess. If that's what it takes for me to not eat alone tonight."

"Are you picking me up or am I picking you up?"

"I'm going to run down to the gym and take a shower. Why don't you pick me up there and we can go somewhere in Midtown?"

"Do you like Tex Mex?"

"Sure."

"Let's go to Escorpion. They have some of the best margaritas."

"Where's that?"

"Near the Fox Theatre."

"I don't know where that is."

"I do. I'll pick you up at seven thirty."

Axel waited outside LA Fitness in Ansley Mall and saw Laura pull into the parking lot. He got in her Mercedes-Benz and threw a small bag with his dirty clothes in the back seat.

Laura pulled back out onto Piedmont Road. She turned on 14th Street, then left onto Peachtree Street until she found a parking lot not far from the restaurant.

"We'll have to walk a couple of blocks."

"No problem. I didn't realize traffic would be this bad tonight."

"This is nothing. You should see it when school is in session, or when there is a concert at the Fox. It's always bad, though."

They walked through the restaurant's front door and waited about 30 minutes for a table. They sat outside on the patio.

"Do you want to split a pitcher of margaritas?" Laura asked.

"I don't drink anymore, Princess."

"You don't?"

"Being in prison sort of forces sobriety on you."

"But you are out now. Drink up!"

"No thanks. You go ahead though."

"Party pooper."

Laura ordered a large margarita. Axel ordered a cola.

Each ordered the taco plates, which came with several tacos and sides. They decided to split sides so they each got different ones. Laura got a second margarita during her meal, making Axel raise an eyebrow.

When they finished, Axel paid the bill and asked for Laura's car keys.

"Why? I'm going to drop you off at the shop."

"Let me drive. Those margaritas looked strong."

"I'm fine, Axel."

"Give me the keys, Princess," Axel said, raising his voice.

"Keep your voice down. You are making a scene."

"You want a scene? I'll make a scene."

"Stop it. Take the fucking keys," she said, throwing her car keys at him.

He bobbled the keys, but eventually closed his fist around them.

Axel got in the driver's seat and moved the seat back. "How do you drive this thing?"

"My legs are shorter than yours."

Axel adjusted the mirrors while Laura frowned. "You are messing up my mirrors."

"You can put them back. I can't even see. Now direct me back to my shop."

Laura gave Axel directions back to Piedmont Road and he knew where he was once he was near Ansley Mall. He pulled into the parking lot and shut off the car.

Laura put out her hand for her keys.

"Come in for a cup of coffee," he said, pulling the keys out of the ignition.

"Give me my keys. I'm ready to go home."

"I'll give them back when you have a cup of coffee," he said, holding them in his fist. She made a feeble attempt to grab them from him, but he pulled his hand back. He looked like he was enjoying keeping them away from her.

"Fine. I'll have a cup of your shitty coffee."

Axel grabbed his clothes bag, then exited the car. He unlocked the side door and Laura huffed into the shop. She tossed her Hermes handbag on the leather couch and sat down hard. "Well, fix me some coffee!"

Axel set up the coffeemaker and pushed start.

"Your wish is my command, Princess."

"Just stop with the princess stuff. It's annoying."

Axel gave her a big grin. "I know."

Laura crossed her arms over her chest.

Axel went back toward his office and suddenly music came over the intercom system. He walked back in the lobby with two ceramic coffee cups.

He poured the coffee into them and handed one to Laura.

"I didn't think you'd want your coffee in Styrofoam."

"I would not." She took the cup and stood up to put sugar in her coffee. "Do you have real cream or milk?"

"I have some in my little refrigerator. I'll go get it."

Axel walked back to his office and took a small carton of milk out of his mini fridge. He handed it to Laura.

She shook it and poured a generous amount in her coffee. She then shook the carton again. "Not much left."

"Guess I won't be having milk with my coffee tomorrow."

"I'll bring you a carton tomorrow."

"I can use the powder stuff."

"That stuff is awful."

Axel shrugged. "I got used to it in prison."

Laura blew on her coffee and took a few sips. "This coffee is terrible. Not even sugar and milk help it."

"Well, that's all we have. Kyle isn't paying for Starbucks."

"But you have a coffee service, right?"

"Yes."

"I think you need a new one."

"I'm not running a coffee shop, Princess. I'm running a service station. We don't need great coffee."

"But you should have better coffee. You'll attract a higher clientele."

"I need better security before I need better coffee. Another cup?"

"Sure. This is garbage, but I want another."

Axel poured more coffee into her cup, refreshed his own, and sat down next to her.

"So why don't you tell me a story about your life."

"My life? How long are you trying to keep me here?"

"Did you have any pets growing up?"

"No. My mother would not have an animal in the house."

"We had dogs at my grandmother's house when I was growing up. They were mostly strays."

"Like you."

Axel ignored her comment. "Do you have any hobbies?"

"You mean answering asinine questions from clients? That's a major hobby."

"Princess, I'm just trying to get to know you."

"You don't need to know me. You don't need to be my friend. I don't need to be yours either. We are work colleagues. That's it."

"Fine. Be that way."

"Now give me my keys."

"Are you OK to drive?"

"I was OK to drive when we left the restaurant, Axel."

Axel handed Laura her keys while she scowled at him. She shoved the door open, got in her car and moved the seat and all the mirrors and drove away from the service station.

Chapter 9

Laura dreaded July 4 in Atlanta. The city held the Peachtree Road Race, which began in Buckhead's Lenox Square and ended 6.2 miles down Peachtree until it ended in Piedmont Park.

Laura had never run the race and hated the event because news and police helicopters began hovering over the start line, waking her up early on the holiday. She did enjoy her balcony view of the fireworks later that night, however.

On this holiday, Laura hated it even more. Her head throbbed because of a broken tooth. The helicopters' beating rotators sounded like they were in her head.

Laura had broken her molar on a Greek salad. The kalamata olive had not been pitted and she bit down hard, breaking the tooth. She broke it on Saturday and couldn't get into her dentist until Friday, three days after July 4. She was lucky to get in at all. Dr. Gabriel was completely booked.

To dull the pain, she'd been drinking lots of wine and downing ibuprofen.

She dreaded the call she would have to make next. Laura's dentist told her she couldn't drive herself home after the dental procedure.

Laura had asked for sedation and Dr. Gabriel said she'd have to have someone else drive her. She could not take an Uber since someone responsible would need to take care of her for 24 hours.

Laura couldn't call Craig. He was no longer in her life. She considered calling Simon. Maybe she could guilt him into that favor. But his wife would never let him stay with her all day and he probably wouldn't want to be away from the restaurant all day, either.

She was going to have to call Axel. He was the only one who might do it. At least it was on a Friday. Surely, he could take the day off. She wouldn't insist he stay over. She could take care of herself.

Laura called Axel midday on July 4.

"I'm off today, like the rest of Atlanta," he said into the phone. "Why are you calling?"

"I need a favor."

"From me? That's a good one, Princess."

"No really. I need a favor."

"What is it?"

"I broke my tooth."

"I run a service station, Princess. You need a dentist to fix that."

"Axel, I'm going to a dentist on Friday, but I can't drive myself there or home. He's going to sedate me, and I need a ride."

"Why can't you take Uber?"

"I asked. I could take an Uber there, but he tells me I have to be released to a responsible person, not an Uber driver."

Axel started to laugh. "That's a good one. Can you repeat that?"

"I need a responsible person, Axel. Unfortunately for me, that would be you."

"What do I get out of it?"

"My undying gratitude, Axel."

"What if I say no?"

"Please don't say no. I'm in a lot of pain here."

"Fine. I'll take you."

"Thank you."

"When is your appointment?"

"Ten in the morning."

"Shit. I'm going to miss work."

"You can drop me off, then go back to work and pick me up when I'm done."

"I'm still going to miss a lot of work. We're busy at the shop."

"I'm sorry. If I had a girlfriend, I would have asked her."

"You don't have any girlfriends?"

"Not here in Atlanta."

"Where are they?"

"I have a friend, Guillerma, in Miami."

"You have one girlfriend, and she's in Miami?"

"Yes."

"I'll pick you up at nine. Don't be late."

Axel texted Laura he was outside her condo building and Laura came out the front door minutes later. Axel could see Laura's face was swollen. She had dark circles under her eyes and looked tired.

"You look rough," he said.

"I haven't been able to sleep much. This pain is awful."

"Why didn't your dentist write you a prescription for the pain?"

"No one's handing out pain medicine anymore. He just told me to take ibuprofen."

Laura gave Axel directions to her dental office. She thought he was just going to drop her off, but he got out and came in with her.

"You don't have to stay. Just come back for me."

"I want to know how long the procedure will take. Then I'll decide if I'm going to stay or come back for you."

Laura checked in with the receptionist and both she and Axel heard the instructions about the procedure, the sedation, and that she'd need care for 24 hours.

"Oh, Princess, you neglected to tell me that part."

"I didn't know that part," she lied. She was angry the receptionist had said that in front of Axel. She was sure she could have taken care of herself after the procedure was over.

"I'm sure you didn't," Axel said, not believing her.

"Listen, I don't need you to watch over me for 24 hours. I'll be fine."

The receptionist interrupted. "You must have a responsible adult to watch you for 24 hours. Just in case you have a reaction to the sedation. You might fall in your home."

"I've never had any kind of reaction," Laura began to say.

"I'll be staying with her," Axel interjected. "Don't worry."

Laura frowned at Axel. "You will not," she hissed.

"I'm staying with you or I'm leaving right now, and you won't get any dental work done today."

"Dammit. Fine."

Axel sat in the dental office's lobby, glancing through the ancient magazines on the coffee table. He picked up the Better Homes & Garden, glowered at the first article on herb gardening, then tossed it back on the table.

There was also a television, but it was tuned to a headline news program.

Two hours later the dental technician opened the door to the lobby and called Axel back.

"Are you her husband?"

Axel snorted out a laugh. "Hardly. I'm just the schmuck who said he'd do her this favor."

"We're going to have to keep her for another hour for observation. She's had a reaction to the sedation."

"Miss I've-Never-Had-A-Reaction had a reaction?"

"She did. She's not feeling very well. Do you have a plastic bucket in case she gets sick on the way home?"

Axel groaned. "I don't. I guess I better go to Walmart and buy one."

"She might not get sick again. She wasn't supposed to eat before today's procedure, but I guess she didn't think coffee was on that list."

"Laura and her coffee," Axel grumbled. "I'll be back. You said I have an hour?"

"We won't release her until you get back so take your time."

Axel got in his truck and regretted they hadn't taken Laura's car. If she puked, he didn't want to smell it in his truck forever. If she puked in his truck he'd probably puke right after her. Even thinking about it made him gag.

Axel pulled into the Walmart parking deck at Howell Mill. He bought several items, including hand towels and paper towels, not just a small bathroom waste can. He hoped he wouldn't have to toss it out of his truck on the drive back to Laura's condo.

He got back to the dentist's office and put the towels, paper towels and waste can in the passenger's seat. The snack items and sodas, which he'd grabbed near the checkout line, he kept in the bag behind his seat.

"She's ready but she's very unsteady on her feet. We'll help you get her into your car."

"Why does she look that way?" he asked the dental tech when he saw Laura.

"She's got cotton in her mouth to keep her from chewing her tongue. They are also covering the stitches."

"She had stitches? For dental work?"

"She did. We had to do a little more than we expected."

The dental tech and Axel had Laura between them and steered her to Axel's truck. He got her situated and put the seat belt around her. Her head flopped to one side. He wasn't so sure she was conscious. How was he going to get her up and into her condo? He had no idea.

He pulled out from the parking lot and back into traffic. Laura suddenly sat up, spitting out one of the pieces of cotton.

"Where am I?" she asked in a muffled voice.

"You are in my truck. I'm taking you back to your place."

"Oh. Is it over?" she asked, pulling out the rest of the cotton from her mouth and dropping it on the floorboard of Axel's truck.

"You're fine, Princess," he said, spying the mess now on the passenger's floor. He swore and muttered, "Never again."

"That's good." Then she closed her eyes and appeared to go back to sleep.

Axel gently nudged Laura after he'd parked in her deck. He was glad she had given him the gate code. He parked right next to her Mercedes-Benz. He hoped his truck wouldn't be ticketed. Surely Laura had told her place he would be there.

Knowing Laura, she probably hadn't mentioned it. He'd have to tell someone. But first he needed her to wake up. What the hell had they given her to sedate her?

He could leave her in the truck for a while, but he didn't want to. What if she puked in his truck while she was alone?

"Laura. Laura, wake up," he said, rubbing her arm. "Please, dear God, wake up!"

Laura's eyes fluttered. She seemed confused.

"Princess, we are back at your place. Let me help you out of the truck. Do you need me to carry you?"

"I'm so tired."

"Let's get you up to your condo. You can go right back to sleep."

"I'm so tired," she repeated.

"Come on. There you go. Hold onto me," he said, holding Laura around the waist. He'd probably have to carry her.

He got her into the building and over to the elevators.

The concierge looked over at them in alarm. "Is Miss Lucas alright? Do you need an ambulance?"

"She's had some oral surgery and has had a reaction to whatever they gave her. I'll keep an eye on her. Listen, I parked my truck next to her car. Will it be OK for the night?"

"Of course, sir," the concierge said, eyeing Axel. "Ours is a gated community."

Gated probably to keep the likes of me out of here, Axel thought darkly.

The elevator opened and Axel pushed the button for the penthouse.

When the elevator door opened again, he asked Laura for her keys. She mumbled something and Axel tried to open her handbag to find them. Instead, her handbag upended, and items fell to the floor of the hallway.

"Ah, shit. Alright, Princess, I'm going to have to put you down."

Axel carefully sat Laura on the carpeting in the hallway, propping her back to the wall. As he bent down to retrieve her keys, Laura slid sideways onto the floor.

Axel opened her front door, then scooped up the contents of her handbag, shoving items back in. He tossed the bag into the condo, hearing it go thud on the wooden floor.

"OK, Princess, now you."

He gathered her off the floor and carried her inside. Axel gave a low whistle when he looked around him. She really was a princess in her tower.

He walked toward the back of the condo, trying to find her bedroom. When he did, he laid Laura down, put a small blanket over her and closed the door behind him.

He went back to the living room to close the front door and eyed the security system next to the door. "What the hell?"

Axel had no idea how to set it and he didn't want to have it go off. He didn't want the cops to come if it did. He simply closed the door and hoped for the best.

Axel realized how hungry he was and opened the refrigerator. It was empty except for some cream, an open bottle of white wine and a few half-empty takeout boxes.

"Well, shit." He'd left his snacks in the trunk. He went back to Laura's bedroom to see if she was still sleeping. She was.

He decided to order a pizza for delivery. He had no idea if Laura would want any or if she could eat after her dental work. He ordered a meat lover's pizza and a 2-liter bottle of soda.

He gave the address, his credit card number, and his cell number.

In about an hour his cell rang. The pizza delivery was outside. Axel put a nearby umbrella in the door so it wouldn't lock behind him and went down to retrieve his pizza. He also got the snacks out of his truck.

He arrived back at the penthouse and put the pizza box on the table. He found a glass and filled it with ice from the ice maker. This was living, he thought. He'd gotten so used to drinking his sodas warm because he didn't have room in his mini fridge for bottles of soda, let alone ice.

Axel polished off half of the pizza and drank half of the soda. He wished he'd ordered more soda. He put the leftover pizza in Laura's refrigerator and tried to figure out how to turn on her television. He hadn't had cable channels since before he went to prison.

Axel found the remote and figured out how to change the channels. But he got bored with the afternoon television talk shows and turned them off.

He looked out at the balcony and decided to refill his soda and sit out there. He wished he'd thought to bring a book. He wondered if Laura had any books. He smiled thinking she probably had a stash of racy romance books somewhere, well hidden.

Her whole place looked like it wasn't really lived in. It was clean and well decorated but devoid of personal accents. No family pictures on the shelves. No trinkets from trips or events. He began to feel sorry for her. Nothing to show she was loved or had loved.

Axel sat out on the balcony for a while but got too hot. He retreated to the air conditioning inside.

Axel wondered why he was so bored. Maybe it was because he didn't think to bring his book or an overnight bag. He'd gotten a library card when he'd moved into the shop. The library didn't check that his was a commercial address. And mail came to him at the shop.

He'd made good use of his card, always finding a mystery or thriller to check out. Lately, he was reading Tom Clancy's spy thrillers. He especially liked the main character, Jack Ryan.

He liked going to the library on Saturday mornings and browsing the shelves. He'd met several homeless people there. He always gave them a few bucks.

If Kyle hadn't set him up with the shop, Axel would have been homeless, too.

Axel once again turned on the television. Maybe he could find a movie to watch.

He finally found "Mission Impossible 3" on HBO. He liked it. The movie had good action. He waited to see what the next movie would be, but it was a romantic comedy. He turned the channel. He didn't want to see a Sandra Bullock movie.

Axel thought he heard a noise from Laura's bedroom and got up to see what it was. He knocked softly on the bedroom door. "Princess? Laura?"

He heard another noise. "Princess, I'm coming in. I'm just going to check on you."

He opened the door to find her with half-opened eyes. The side of her face looked bruised and swollen.

"Are you OK?"

"Pain," she mouthed.

"Did the dentist give you a prescription for the pain?"

She shook her head and began to cry.

"Where is your Tylenol?"

Laura tried to sit up but couldn't. She just pointed toward the master bathroom.

"I'll find it."

Axel went in and looked around. The bathroom was as neat as the rest of Laura's home. No toothpaste on the counter, no hair brush or toothbrush. He began pulling out drawers and opening the cabinets under the sinks.

He finally found what he was looking for. He opened the bottle and put two capsules in his hand. He handed them to Laura. "I'll get you some water."

He got a glass of water from the kitchen and handed it to her. She took it and tried to swallow the pills, but she couldn't. "Do you have a straw?" he asked.

Laura shook her head and let him know she did not.

Axel sat down on the edge of the bed and propped her up. "Give me the glass. Take small sips."

Laura took smaller sips and finally was able to swallow the pain pills. "More," she whispered.

"Here," he said, holding the glass up to her lips.

Laura shook her head. "More pills."

"I gave you two."

"Two more," she whispered. "Please."

Axel went back to the bathroom and returned with another two capsules.

She took them and he helped her to sip the water until she swallowed those as well.

Laura laid back down. Axel sat on the edge of the bed again.

"Are you hungry at all? I have pizza."

Laura made a face at him.

"Yeah, well, I wanted pizza. I can order soup or something. Is there a Chinese place nearby?"

Laura shook her head. "Not hungry."

"I'll let you sleep."

Laura closed her eyes and nodded her head. "Thank you," she mouthed.

Chapter 10

Axel watched more television and checked on Laura every hour. She was still sleeping soundly.

He stood in her bedroom doorway. She even looks like a sleeping princess, he thought. Black hair, pouty lips. She was beautiful, except for the swelling and slight bruising on her face right now. Axel shook his head to clear thoughts of her.

He went back into the kitchen and finished off the leftover pizza and the soda. He thought about going out for more soda, but he didn't want to leave Laura alone. He'd have to stick to water for the rest of the evening. He didn't stay up late. He was tired and bored.

Axel found the guest bedroom and bathroom. He decided to take a nice hot shower before he retired. He never showered that long at the gym.

At Laura's home, he did. He toweled off with clean-smelling towels and got ready for bed. Axel usually slept in his boxer shorts, but he didn't want to go into Laura's bedroom to check on her one last time in just his shorts.

He wrapped the towel around his waist and opened the door to check on her. He was surprised to see her sitting upright in bed looking right at him.

"Laura, are you OK?"

"Axel?"

"I just came to check on you before I went to bed. Do you need more pain pills?"

"Why are you in my towel?"

"I just took a shower. Figured your shower would be nicer than the gym."

"And?"

"And it was. You have lots of hot water. If you don't need anything, I'll just be heading to bed."

"But I do need something."

"What?"

"You."

Axel froze and stood silent, then returned to the guest bedroom, closing Laura's door behind him.

Axel couldn't sleep after Laura's words. She said she needed him. What did that mean? Was she sleepwalking? Was he dreaming? Was it the extra pain killers she'd taken making her loopy? Maybe she was still under the influence of the sedation she'd had.

Axel laid in the dark for a long while. It was quiet in the penthouse. He couldn't hear street noise. That was the first thing he'd noticed about sleeping in the shop.

Cars roared by even in the dead of night. He'd even heard occasional gunshots. Axel learned to sleep lightly.

In the penthouse, it was almost too quiet. If he listened closely, he could almost make out muffled street noise and a car horn. Axel rolled over in the queen-sized bed. It felt so much better than his full-sized air mattress. He finally drifted off into a deep sleep.

Axel was startled awake by a woman screaming. He instinctively reached under the mattress for his gun. But it wasn't there because he wasn't in his shop.

He bolted out of the guest bedroom and heard the screams coming from Laura's bedroom. He opened the door, ready to tackle anyone who was in there harming her.

Laura was sobbing in her bed, the room empty.

"Laura! What happened?"

She could barely catch her breath. "Julio. I saw Julio."

Axel looked around, then realized she meant her ex-boyfriend. "You said he's dead, Laura."

"He was right here, in my room." She put her face in her hands and cried harder.

Axel sat on the edge of her bed and put his arms around her. "I'm here. You're safe."

Laura threw her arms around Axel and cried as if her heart were broken. He gently stroked her hair trying to soothe her sobs.

Axel attempted to straighten up, but Laura clung to him. She wouldn't let go. "Don't leave me," she pleaded. "Please stay."

"Laura, I don't think I should."

"Please, Axel. Sleep next to me. I'll feel better if you do."

"I'll be right back."

Axel went back to the guest bedroom and put his jeans back on. He didn't plan to sleep next to Laura in just his boxers. He could already feel his penis beginning to harden. Think sad thoughts, think sad thoughts, he kept telling himself.

He knocked before entering her bedroom.

"Come in," she said.

Axel entered to find Laura under the covers. She appeared to have undressed.

"Wouldn't you be more comfortable in a nightgown or something?" he asked.

"No. Would you?"

"I'll just sleep over here," he said, lying on the far side of her bed.

Axel laid ramrod straight in the bed, not touching Laura, trying not to even look at her. She rolled over and he could feel her nipple against his arm.

Think sad thoughts. Think sad thoughts, he kept repeating.

"Thank you for helping me today," she whispered. "I appreciate it."

"It's fine," he said. "Happy to help."

Laura began to stroke his chest.

Sad thoughts, sad thoughts, Axel kept repeating. It wasn't working. His smaller head had a mind of its own tonight.

"I'd like to show you how much I appreciate it," she whispered.

"Princess, I think we should just go to sleep."

"Are you sleepy? Because I'm not."

"Then why don't you tell me about your dream? Why are you dreaming of Julio?"

Laura frowned. "Why would you ask me that?" she asked angrily. She sat up, the sheet dropping down, exposing her bare breasts.

Axel looked away. "I just want to know why you are dreaming about your ex-boyfriend."

"I'm not dreaming about him," she shouted. "I'm having nightmares about him."

"Why?" '

"Because he raped me!" she shouted. "That's why my brother killed him. And then the drug gang killed my brother. At least that's what I think happened."

Laura got out of bed, storming around her bedroom, naked, angry, and crying. Axel clambered out of bed too, hoping Laura wouldn't notice the strain in his jeans.

"I'm sorry. I didn't know."

"He beat me and raped me. I was just a girl! A girl! I can still feel his hands around my neck!"

Axle wrapped his arms around Laura. Her skin was so soft. He touched her hair and stroked her face, wiping away her tears.

Laura's breathing became more even. She melted into his arms, spent.

"I'm so tired, Axel. I'm just so tired." Tears began to spill once more.

"Let's get you back to bed. I'll get you some water. Do you want to take some more pain medicine?"

Laura shook her head. "Give me the nighttime pain medicine. I don't want to dream anymore tonight."

Axel went back into her bathroom and found the pain reliever with a sleeping aid. He gave her two pills and then got some water from the kitchen.

When he got back to the bedroom, Laura was tucked under the covers. She sat up, swallowed the pills, and laid back down.

"Will you still sleep next to me?"

"Sure, Princess. I'll make sure you are safe tonight."

Axel awoke the next morning with Laura pressed up against him, her head tucked under his shoulder. He tried to move. He needed to get up and use the bathroom.

Axel tried to slide out of the bed without waking Laura, but she began to stir.

He got out of bed and went to the guest bathroom. When he was done, he splashed cold water on his face. He needed to stay strong and not be weak around Laura. But she was making it difficult.

Axel was startled by a knock on the bathroom door. "Axel?"

"I'll be out in a minute. Just freshening up."

"I woke up and you weren't there."

"I'll be right out, OK?" he said, irritation in his voice.

"OK," she said, softly. "Do you want some coffee?"

Axel sighed. He didn't want to be angry with her. And she sounded like she was trying to be nice.

Axel went back to his bedroom and quickly pulled on his shirt, then went out to the kitchen. Laura, wrapped in a robe, was in front of her cafetera making the first cup of Cuban coffee.

"That smells good."

"It's my good coffee. Not that crap in your shop. Here is the first cup. Do you want sugar and cream?"

"Just cream. That's about all you have in your refrigerator."

"I need to go to the store," she said.

"I guess I'm just having coffee for breakfast today," Axel said, saluting Laura with his coffee mug.

"There might be some fruit."

"Not in that refrigerator. Unless it magically grew there overnight."

Laura began making her own cup of coffee, dumping sugar and cream into her cup.

She sat down at the kitchen table across from Axel. "Sorry about breakfast."

"It's alright. I'll grab something later this morning."

"We could go out for breakfast. I'll get dressed."

Laura disappeared into her bedroom and came out in a cotton blouse and her leather miniskirt. Her hair was up in a messy bun, and she was putting on her high heels.

"We need to go somewhere where I won't be recognized. My face is still a bit swollen."

"Will you be able to eat?"

"I'm not sure. But I am hungry. Maybe I can eat scrambled eggs. I'll drive."

"Princess, I'll drive. You had a bad reaction to that sedation. I don't want you to pass out while you are driving."

"I'm not going to pass out."

"I'm driving and that's final."

"Fine. You drive."

Axel opened the passenger door for Laura, who climbed in. "Why is there a wastebasket on the floor?"

"That was in case you puked in the truck," he answered, starting the truck, and pulling out onto Peachtree Road.

"What?"

"Apparently you puked at the dentist's office. They told me to go get a plastic bucket in case you puked on the way home. I got this instead. I can probably use it at the shop."

"I don't remember being sick."

"I doubt you remember much of anything. You were out of it."

"I wasn't sick in your truck, was I?"

"If you had puked in my truck I'd have puked right after you and then you and the waste can would have been tossed out the window."

"Gee, thanks."

"Where am I going?"

"Let's go to Flying Biscuit in Midtown. I know they have scrambled eggs."

"If all you want is scrambled eggs, let's go right down the street to IHOP. I want a big stack of pancakes."

"IHOP? Who the hell goes to IHOP?"

"I do. It's a cheap breakfast."

"Cheap doesn't mean good."

"You are having scrambled eggs, Princess. Do you want them with fancy cheese or something?"

"No."

"Do you think anyone will recognize you there?"

"Probably not. I never go there."

"IHOP it is, Princess."

Laura had never seen a man eat that much breakfast. Axel ordered a large stack of pancakes then ordered eggs, bacon, hash browns and coffee. Laura just ordered eggs, hash browns and coffee and ate all of them painfully slow.

"I guess you were hungry," she said.

"Hey, I usually have snacks in the shop. I am hungry."

"What kind of snacks do you eat? Chips and junk like that?"

"No, Princess. I usually keep nuts, apples, bananas, and other fresh fruit."

"You must go to the store a lot."

"Just once a week, maybe twice if I need more fruit. Unlike you, I stock up on snacks. I may get take out or go to a restaurant and eat at the bar for my meals, but I always have snacks," he said, pointing at Laura with his fork. "What you have in your refrigerator wouldn't keep a mouse alive."

As they finished up breakfast, Laura took out her credit card to pay the bill. "Let me get this, to thank you for helping me yesterday."

"Oh no, Princess," Axel said, putting his hand over hers. "I'm getting this. When you thank me, it cost more than just a cheap breakfast. I want a steak dinner."

Laura rolled her eyes at him. Axel took several bills out of his pocket and left them on the table.

"Ready to head home?" he asked.

"We could do something today."

"Together?"

"Yes, together. Want to go to a movie or something?"

"Princess, it's not even ten o'clock."

"There might be a matinee. When was the last time you went to the movies?"

"Over four years ago."

"That long?"

Axel gave Laura a withering look.

"Oh, right. Guess they didn't have movie nights in prison, huh?"

"We had movies, but they weren't new movies. They were screened before we could watch them. No sex, no violence, no fun. I watched 'Mission Impossible 3' on your cable last night. I liked that there were guns and violence and things blowing up."

"We could go back to my place and watch movies there if you want."

"You don't have any snacks."

"Oh, for fuck's sake, stop at the store and I'll buy you some snacks!" Laura said, exasperated. "You're like a toddler!"

"How would you know? Your place doesn't look like you've ever had kids in it."

"I should certainly hope not. Kids are disgusting germ factories."

Axel laughed. "You're the real mothering type, huh?"

"Hey, you don't strike me as the father type either."

"What makes you say that?" Axel asked defensively. "I want to be a father. I think I'd make a great father."

"A father who has kids that never puke."

"It's because a kid at my school puked on me one time," Axel said, starting to gag. "And then I puked all over myself. Jesus, I can't even think about it. It's going to make me sick."

"Don't think about it then! Pull into the grocery store and let's get some snacks for you."

"You should get some snacks and food for you, too."

"I'll just get a rotisserie chicken and some sides. That will hold me for the rest of the weekend."

"Will you be able to chew chicken?"

"If I cut it up small."

"You better get some soup, too."

About an hour later, Axel and Laura left the grocery store with bags filled with fruit, bagged snacks, several deli sides, the rotisserie chicken, cans of soup, and bottles of soda, and wine.

They put the grocery bags on Laura's kitchen counter.

"Hey, I probably should be getting back to the shop. A couple of the guys are working today on a car by themselves and some of them definitely need supervision."

"What are you going to do for the rest of the weekend by yourself? Stay here with me."

"Well, I only expected to stay overnight for one night. I need clean clothes, to do laundry, you know, normal stuff."

"Bring your laundry here. I have a machine and dryer. Bring your own laundry stuff. I don't think I have any left."

"Princess, I bet you never even use your washer and dryer."

"I do too!"

Axel arched an eyebrow. "Really?"

"Well, no. I usually bring my clothes to the dry cleaners. I wash my delicates in the sink."

"If you are offering, I'd love to do my laundry here. Laundromats are so boring."

"So go check on your techs, then come back with your stuff. By the time you get back, it will be time for dinner."

"See you soon, then," he said.

Chapter 11

Axel got back to the shop, letting himself into the empty space. The guys were gone. It didn't look like they had been working on the car at all. They probably didn't even come in, he thought and then frowned.

The shop still wasn't open on Saturdays yet. He imagined if business kept increasing, he would have to hire a couple more technicians and open for limited hours on Saturday. Then they would have to show up and work.

Right now, he enjoyed the quiet of the cavernous space. He began to gather his laundry and then began having second thoughts about returning to Laura's condo.

Was it a ploy? Did she really want something more from him? Did he want more from her? Was he willing to go down that road with her? Was he willing to have this just be a one-night stand? Or was he getting ahead of himself?

Or was this just a friendly gesture on her part? Maybe this was just one friend allowing another friend to do laundry. Axel laughed inwardly at his own thoughts. When did Laura offer a friendly gesture? Laura was the embodiment of ulterior motives.

Still, he did want to do laundry at her place. He could watch TV and eat snacks and do a chore he dreaded every week.

He loaded his laundry basket, put his latest Tom Clancy book on top of the pile, put two condoms in his back pocket, and got back in his truck and headed to Laura's condo.

Laura buzzed Axel back into the parking deck. She paced nervously around her condo. While Axel was away, she showered, blew dry her hair, and applied makeup.

She opened her closet and pulled out a pair of faded jeans she rarely wore and a dark pink cotton blouse. She tried to think when the last time was that she wore this outfit. She remembered it was out in

Napa. But she did put on her heels. Axel was so much taller than she. Laura wanted to look nice when he arrived.

Axel knocked on her door and Laura undid her extra security, then opened it. Axel could hear the mechanical lock opening.

"That was quick," she said as he entered. "I wasn't expecting you back until later this afternoon."

"The guys were gone. I don't think they showed up this morning."

"I'm sure you'll yell at them on Monday."

"What's with all the extra security? Who are you trying to keep out?" he asked.

"I just feel safer with the extra security."

"Why? Has the building ever had break-ins?

"Never. And I'd like to keep it that way."

Axel shrugged. "Where can I put this?" he asked, his laundry basket in his hands.

"Here you go," Laura said, opening some louvered doors that hid the washing machine and dryer.

"I'll just get the first load started," he said, opening the washer and putting his towels and bed sheets in.

"Great. We can have lunch. Have you eaten? Are you hungry? I am. Must have been because I didn't eat at all yesterday. I'll just reheat the chicken."

"Are you sure you can chew it?"

"I'll cut it up into small pieces. I should be fine. The coleslaw and potato salad are small enough already. I should be able to eat those just fine."

"You should have gotten the baked beans. Those are small. You could have eaten those easily."

"There is a reason I didn't get the beans."

"Oh, you don't want to fart all night?"

Laura made a face at Axel. "A woman doesn't fart. She passes gas."

"Well excuse me, Princess. We men fart." Just then, Axel let out a loud fart.

Laura screwed up her lips and waved her hand in front of her face. "You're disgusting."

Axel gave her a big smile. "Yes, I am."

"Wipe that silly grin off your face. I'm going to heat up the food."

Laura put the chicken, still in its bag, in the microwave and hit the reheat setting. She took out some spoons and put them in the deli containers. She also pulled down some plates and put them on the table. She got a wine glass down for herself and a drinking glass for Axel.

"You're sure you don't want a beer? I have some from when Troy... Ah when a friend was here."

"Soda will be fine for me, thanks. Now, who was Troy?"

"Just a friend," Laura said. The microwave buzzer went off and Laura took the chicken out and placed it on the counter.

"You are a terrible liar, Princess. I'm guessing he was a friend with benefits."

Laura blushed. "If you must know, he was. But that's over. He's moved on and so have I."

"Who's the lucky man these days?"

"I'm between boyfriends at the moment. Why? Do you want the job?"

"You mean if I don't mind being chewed up, spit out, and tossed out like yesterday's trash? Then yeah, sign me up."

Laura looked at Axel, furious. "Get out!" she shouted, pointing toward the door.

"What? Now? My stuff is in the washing machine!"

"When it is done, you need to leave."

"And you need to calm the hell down, Princess," he shouted back, pointing at Laura.

"Stop calling me that!" she yelled, getting close to Axel. He was still nearly a foot taller, but she stood on her tiptoes to make herself taller and balled up her fists as if to strike him. "I don't like that name! My name is Laura."

"Well, I'll stop calling you Princess when you stop acting like one!" Axel yelled back.

Laura grabbed Axel by the arms and began trying to shake him. He barely moved.

"Ahhhh," she shouted in her frustration. "You bastard!"

Axel wrapped his arms around her, holding her close to his body. He could smell her hair, her perfume, her rage.

"Stop it, Princess. Just stop it before you hurt yourself."

Laura looked up at Axel, tears in her angry eyes. She moved her arms to his neck and pulled his face down toward hers. He bent down and kissed her. She kissed him back harder. His tongue sought hers.

His hands ran down her back and settled on her waist. He could feel her heat.

Laura stood back and ran her hand down the front of his jeans. Axel could feel himself becoming aroused.

"Oh, Princess, don't start something you don't intend to finish," he murmured.

"I think you want this as much as I do," she said.

"That's not what I said."

"Come," she said, taking his hand and leading him into the bedroom.

Laura started to undress, but Axel put his hand around her wrist and pulled it away from her clothing. "Allow me," he said.

He began to unbutton her blouse slowly, one button at a time. Then he slid it off her shoulders, allowing it to fall to the floor. When Axel's fingertips brushed her shoulders, she felt a shock of electricity go through her body.

Next, he ran his fingers around the waistband of her jeans until he got to the front. He unbuttoned her jeans and pulled down the zipper.

Laura bit her lip. The anticipation was excruciating.

"Take off those ridiculous heels, Princess."

Laura quickly kicked off her shoes. She sat down on the bed and Axel grabbed the legs of her jeans and pulled them off.

Laura sat in her black lace bra and thong. "Now you," she said, reaching for the waistband of his jeans.

Axel stepped back from Laura and took off each of his shoes, then stood back in front of her.

She unbuttoned his fly and ran her finger around his bulging penis. Axel blew out a long breath.

Laura pulled down his pants and Axel helped her take them off. Next, she pulled his polo shirt over his head. She ran her hands down his muscular shoulders and arms. She could feel a bit of dampness between her legs.

Axel pushed her down on the bed, rubbing his face between her breasts. He inhaled deeply.

"That would be better if you took off my bra."

"In good time, Princess. I don't want to rush."

Laura arched her back when he began to suck her nipples through the lacing of her bra. She made small moans. Axel then gently bit one nipple. Laura's intake of breath was audible.

Axel began rubbing his hand on the outside of Laura's panties. He could feel a bit of dampness on the fabric.

Laura arched her back again. She was so ready for Axel to be inside her. "Please, Axel, please."

"Not yet, Princess. Not yet."

"I want," she panted. "I want you."

"I know what you want."

Axel reached behind her back and unsnapped her bra, pulling it away from her body. He laid down next to her, feeling her soft smooth skin next to his as he began to lick and suck her nipples, feeling them get erect under his tongue.

Laura arched her back again, wrapping her legs around one of his. She started rubbing her thong underwear up and down his leg.

Axel reached down and put his fingers under the fabric, beginning to play with her labia.

"Oh God, Axel! I'm going to cum!"

"Easy, Princess. Easy."

Laura couldn't hold back any longer. She had a strong orgasm at just the touch of his fingertips around her.

Laura balled her fists up again, almost angry with Axel. "I wanted you to be inside me."

"Patience, Princess. I'm not done yet."

She looked at him with his toothy grin. She wanted to smack him.

Axel got on his knees on the bed and removed her thong, now wetter than before. Laura could see a distinct outline of his penis under his boxers. Jesus, she thought, he's big. She began to feel aroused again.

"Let me take yours off," she said.

Axel shuffled on his knees closer to her and she pulled his boxers down. His penis sprang up, erect.

"Now let's have some fun," she said, grasping his shaft and beginning to rub it. She got on her knees and bent to take it in her mouth, but Axel stopped her.

"No, not now."

Laura looked at him quizzically. Didn't all guys long for a blowjob? Confused, Laura kept stroking his shaft, then used her thumbnail to run over the sensitive head. Now it was Axel's turn to gasp.

A little bit of semen seeped out. Laura used it to rub all over the head of his shaft.

"Oh, God. I'm ready."

Laura got on her back and Axel rolled on top of her. She bent her knees and Axel slipped inside her. Laura's eyes got wide at how tight she was around his big dick.

Axel began a smooth rhythmic stroke inside her. Laura could feel her orgasm begin to build again.

Axel grunted with every stroke and Laura tried to stifle her moans. She was afraid she was going to scream when she came for a second time.

"Axel. Axel. Axel," she repeated. "I'm …."

Suddenly Axel roared his orgasm, shoving hard inside Laura. She screamed with pleasure.

The couple lay on the bed, sweaty and panting.

Laura could feel tears in her eyes. She'd never cried after sex. Ever. But she felt such a release of emotions with Axel.

"Are you alright?" he asked, concerned. He rolled over to face her. "Did I hurt you?"

"No, no," she said, quickly wiping her tears. "I don't know why I'm crying. It felt so good."

Axel pulled Laura closer to him, wrapping her up in his arms. The pair fell asleep soon after.

They awoke hours later. Laura had nuzzled under Axel's shoulder again, her hand draped on his chest.

Axel tried to stretch his legs, then his arms and Laura stirred next to him.

"Good afternoon, Princess," he said.

"Good afternoon, lover."

"What's that smell?"

"Smell?"

"I smell chicken."

"Oh shit! The chicken!"

Laura quickly scrambled out of bed. Axel could hear the refrigerator door open and close.

Laura then returned to the bed. "Well, we might not be able to eat that chicken or we'll both end up with food poisoning."

"I don't think so, either. You know how I feel about puking."

Laura couldn't help but laugh. Then she turned serious.

"Am I the first woman you've been with since you got out of prison?"

"Don't flatter yourself, Princess. I hooked up with an old girlfriend when I got out. But it was a pity fuck on her part. I knew it wouldn't last."

"So that old girlfriend is here in Atlanta?"

"Why? Jealous?"

"No," she said. Laura frowned. She *was* going to be jealous of his old girlfriend if she was here in Atlanta.

Axel pulled her close to him again.

"You are really a terrible liar, Princess. Remind me to play poker with you."

"Is she here in Atlanta?"

"No, she lives in South Georgia. It was a one-and-done." Axel was quiet for a moment. "I hope this isn't a one-and-done."

"I hope not either," she said, snuggling into him. "What are we going to do for dinner?"

"We can order another pizza."

"I guess we will have to. I'm hungry. Or we could go out." She looked up to see his reaction.

"Princess, I just want to stay here with you."

"Alright then, I'll order pizza. I'm starving. What do you want on your half?"

"Half? I want a whole pizza. Meat lovers. You get whatever you want on your pizza. And order some more soda too."

Axel saw the frown forming on Laura's face.

"Please."

"That's more like it."

She got out of bed and went into the kitchen where she had left her cellphone. She came back to the bedroom and put in a call for delivery. "Medium meat lovers," she began to order until Axel mouthed the word large. "Make that a large meat lovers pizza. And I want a medium pepperoni with mushrooms and black olives."

"And soda," Axel reminded her.

"And two 2-liters of Coke."

Laura waited while the young woman read her order back to her. Laura gave her address, cell number, and credit card number. "Thank you."

She turned to Axel, smiling. "She says it will be about an hour. What shall we do until then?"

"You look like you have some ideas."

"Oh, I do."

Chapter 12

They had just finished making love when Laura's cellphone rang. Axel offered to go down to get the pizzas and sodas. Axel quickly dressed and went to the elevator.

Laura got up, put on her robe, and went to the kitchen to pour herself a glass of wine. She pulled out a bottle of the Cabernet she loved.

Then she went to the washing machine and put Axel's towels and sheets in the dryer.

Axel, with his hands full, could only tap the door with his foot. Laura opened the door for him and then went about setting the security system.

"I feel like I'm back in prison," Axel said, watching her set the alarm.

"Well, you aren't."

Axel put the pizza on the counter. He grabbed his drinking glass and filled it with ice then opened one of the soda bottles. The top made a familiar hiss as he opened it.

"You're having wine?"

"Yes. There's more than enough if you want a glass."

"I'm good. Cheers," he said, tapping her wine glass with his soda glass. "Let's eat. My mouth was watering in the elevator."

Laura and Axel enjoyed the pizza. The delivery had included some chocolate chip cookies.

Axel ate half of the large pizza while Laura had only two slices of her medium.

"Hey, can we watch a movie tonight?" he asked.

"A movie? I had some other activities planned."

"Princess, I'm not a young man anymore. I need to wait a while for your other activities."

"You should take some Viagra."

"I will not. I want what happens to come naturally."

Laura giggled.

"What's so funny?"

"You said come naturally."

Axel grinned at her. "You have a dirty mind, Princess."

"I think you like that."

"Listen, we didn't exactly chat before sex. I didn't use a condom."

"You don't have to. I'm on the pill." This time Laura was telling the truth.

"Have you ever taken an HIV test?"

"Why the hell would I ever do that?" she asked angrily.

"I'm not judging you. I think you've had a lot of boyfriends. I want us both to be safe. I've had one. I'm clean."

"Well, I'm clean too," she said.

"Princess, you really are a horrible liar."

Laura burst into tears. "I'm not lying. I got one last year after I got pregnant."

Laura's hand flew to her mouth, her eyes wide.

"I didn't mean to tell you that," she said.

"But no baby?"

"No," she said softly. "I miscarried."

Laura wiped her eyes. "I didn't want it anyway. The guy was married. Or separated, but he eventually went back to his wife. It just saved me the trouble of getting rid of it."

"Oh, Princess. But it was a life."

"Don't 'oh Princess' me and get all holier than thou. There was no way I would have kept that baby. The man was married. He said he didn't want to be a father and I sure as hell don't want to be a mother."

Axel sighed. The conversation made him sad.

"Let's watch a movie then," he said, changing the subject.

Laura poured another glass of wine and sat on the couch, away from Axel.

"Are you mad at me now? You won't sit next to me?"

"I *am* mad at you. I don't know why I tell you such personal things about me. It's like you have this power to make me say things I don't want to."

"What are you talking about? What things?"

"I told you about Julio. I told you about my miscarriage. I don't want to tell you any more about me."

Axel shrugged and turned on the television. "Suit yourself. I'm an open book. You can ask me anything."

"OK, mister open book. Why did you start dealing drugs?"

Axel now picked up the remote and turned off the TV.

"You are really hung up about that aren't you?"

"I'm not hung up about it. I want to know something personal about you."

"Something personal? I'll tell you something personal. Prison was no piece of cake, Princess. It still haunts me. At night I could hear grown men crying, knowing they were being sexually abused by other men in their cells."

Laura sat still. "No one ever tried to do that to you, did they?"

"Of course, they did. That's why I had to get the HIV test."

Axel stood up and began pacing in front of the TV. "You have nightmares about Julio. I have nightmares about that. Two men holding me down, while another…"

He couldn't say more. Laura could see the pain in his face.

"I'm sorry," Laura whispered.

"You're not the only broken person in this room," Axel said, his voice cracking.

Laura got up from the couch and went over to him, hugging him hard. Axel began to weep.

He pulled Laura's head into his chest. They rocked back and forth in the living room for several minutes. Then Axel pulled away.

"Jesus. I've never told anyone that. Not even Kyle knows."

"I'm sorry I got mad at you. We can watch the movie if you want."

"I'm not in the mood now."

"I'll put on some music."

Laura turned out the lights and found a soft rock channel on Spotify and sat back on the couch. "Here," she said, patting the space next to her, "sit next to me."

Axel sat next to her, and Laura took his hand, entwining her fingers with his. Next, she leaned into him. Axel closed his eyes. They both fell asleep on the couch.

Laura woke first, trying to move her arm. It had fallen asleep, and it was behind Axel. She was stuck and her arm began to burn.

"Axel," she said. He didn't move. "Axel," she said louder.

That startled him awake. "What? What's the matter," he said, trying to get to his feet. But his leg was asleep as well and he stumbled, then landed hard on the floor.

"You were sleeping on my arm, and it fell asleep. It feels like it's on fire," she said, rubbing her right arm. "Are you OK?"

"I'll be OK," he said, sitting for a moment and rubbing his neck. "My leg fell asleep too. Do you have any more ibuprofen? My back and neck are killing me."

"I'll get us both some. We shouldn't have fallen asleep on the couch."

Laura felt her way in the darkness to her bedroom and turned on the light. She went to the bathroom and came back with the pill bottle.

"How many do you want?"

"Just two." Axel got on his knees and then stood up. He walked gingerly on the leg that had fallen asleep into the kitchen and got his glass of cola. He popped the pills into his mouth and swallowed a gulp of the soda. "Yuck. It's warm."

"What time is it?" Laura asked but looked over at the clock on the microwave. "Oh. We really slept. It's two in the morning."

Laura took her two pills but washed them down with the last of her wine.

"We should probably go to bed."

"As long as it isn't as uncomfortable as that couch. Even the beds in prison were better than that."

"I wouldn't know. I've never slept on it before tonight."

"Jesus, my back hurts."

"Let me get you to bed then."

"Princess, I might be out of commission tonight."

"Oh no, you don't. You lay on your back, and I'll do all the work."

Axel grinned at her. "Now that's my kind of woman."

For the second time that Sunday Laura and Axel awoke in each other's arms. Laura awoke first. She tried to slip out of bed, but Axel didn't want to let her go.

"Why is it still dark in here?"

"I have blackout curtains. Here, close your eyes for a moment."

Laura pushed a small button on the wall near her bed and the curtains began to open electronically.

Axel had covered his eyes with his hand and blinked into the now bright room.

"I see why you have those curtains. Damn it's bright out. Oh hell."

"What is it?"

"I never finished doing my laundry."

"Finish it today. I'll go make us some coffee."

Laura went into the kitchen smiling. She had indeed done all the work last night, but she enjoyed it. She liked being on top now and again. She felt like she was more in control.

Axel had fondled her breasts as she rocked back and forth on him. He nearly bucked her off the bed when he finally came. And he didn't complain once about his back hurting.

Axel entered the kitchen and Laura handed him the first cup of coffee.

"That's a fancy contraption for just one cup of coffee. And it looks like you need a new one."

"It's called a cafetera and it was my grandmother's. She brought it over from Cuba."

"Is that where your family is from?"

"Yes."

But you don't have a Hispanic last name. Did someone marry an American?"

"Our family name was Lopez, but my grandfather changed it. Wanted it to sound more American."

"Hmm. This coffee is good. Thank your grandmother for me."

"Oh, she's been gone a while. My grandfather died first. She died several years after him."

"Were you close to her?"

"I guess I was. She was strict though. I always had to wear dresses and I couldn't get them dirty in any way. I wanted a pair of shorts in the worst way. All my friends were allowed to wear them. I was not. She said it was a sin to show that much leg."

"But if you wore a dress you could see your legs."

"I had to keep them covered with white tights. In Miami!"

"It sounds like she was very old-fashioned."

"She was," Laura said, sipping her own cup of coffee. Laura was lost in thought about her grandmother. "She smelled like gardenias."

"What?"

"She had this perfume. It wasn't perfume though. It was eau de toilette. Cheaper than perfume and it smelled like gardenias. She wore it every day," Laura said, standing against her kitchen counter lost in the memory. She took a sip of her own sweetened coffee. "When I smell gardenias, I think of her."

"That's nice."

"What was your grandmother like?"

"She was just as strict as yours. But she believed in not sparing the rod, so I got my ass whipped a lot."

"Did you deserve it?"

"Not always, Princess, not always."

"I'm sorry. You don't have good memories of her?"

"They aren't all bad. This one time she let me go out hunting with her."

"Hunting?"

"Yeah. For deer."

"Deer? Like Bambi?"

"We don't name them, Princess. Anyway, we were on land we shouldn't have been, and she knew it. I shot this buck, but it wasn't a clean kill, and it ran into the woods. She made me run after it. I finally got to it. It was lying in the woods and this guy was next to it trying to say he'd shot it. He was trying to claim it."

"What happened?"

"What happened is my grandmother finally caught up with me and she had her rifle trained on that guy. She said she would shoot him in the woods, and they'd never find his body. She was not going to let him claim that buck. That was our food for the better part of the fall and winter."

"Holy shit! She sounds like a badass."

"She was. She died while I was in prison. I didn't get to go to her funeral."

"I'm sorry."

"Yeah, what are you going to do? Even if I could have gone to her funeral, I wouldn't have. She disowned me after I went to prison. Kyle is my only family now."

"What about your mother?"

"I have no idea where she is. She left me with my grandmother when I was still a baby and took off. I really don't remember her. She could be dead for all I know. Really," Axel said, looking away from Laura. "She is dead to me."

Laura put her cup of coffee down and hugged Axel.

"I told you last night you weren't the only broken person in the room."

"We're not broken," she said, looking up at him. "We are fighters. We are strong because of it."

Axel snorted. "You should put that on a coffee cup," he said. "You could make millions like Kyle."

Laura made a face at him. "Fuck you, Axel."

"Is that an insult or a suggestion?"

Laura gave him a big grin. "A suggestion, I think."

Chapter 13

Laura couldn't remember the last time she'd enjoyed a weekend so much. She was sorry when it finally ended.

She and Axel had made love several times that weekend, and each time she seemed to have a stronger orgasm than the one before.

They had told each other secrets they never shared with others.

Laura realized she didn't despise the man anymore. During that weekend, she had grown quite fond of him. She felt she had come to understand a little more about him.

Laura did feel a little bit guilty about breaking her promise to Kyle to not sleep with another of his clients. She tried not to think of Axel as Kyle's client, so much as his family.

Kyle probably wouldn't like that either. But what was the meaning of life, if not living and loving it, fully?

Axel had stayed over Sunday night, leaving her place Monday before sunrise to get ready to open the shop. Laura could still smell his aftershave on her sheets after he left. She had derided the scent once. Now it turned her on.

She couldn't wait to get to Axel's Motors that morning. She could have worked at home that day, but she wanted to see Axel.

They had talked Sunday evening about how they'd have to be careful around each other. Axel said he didn't want to be paranoid, but he thought one of his technicians might also be feeding information about him to Kyle.

"Then fire him," Laura had said.

"Kyle will just find some other mole. Besides, he's a good mechanic."

Laura frowned. She wondered if he did that after her affair with Simon. It might have been as much about keeping tabs on her as well as Axel.

Laura pulled into the parking lot but parked slightly down from Axel's truck. She came in smiling, asking where Axel was.

A technician pointed to his office. She knocked on the door and Axel said, "Come."

"Don't mind if I do," Laura said softly.

"Princess, what did we talk about?" he asked in hushed tones. "I don't think you should be here."

"But I have work to do."

"You can do it at your place. Don't come here."

Laura looked hurt and surprised. "Are you banning me from the shop?" she asked loudly.

Axel raised his voice. "I've had enough of your fancy pants in my shop."

Laura's eyes grew wide.

"Just play along," he whispered, and nodded toward the door.

"I'm leaving!" she shouted. "But are you coming over tonight?" she asked in a whisper.

Axel smiled. "Good! Now get the hell out!" he said loudly. "I'll see you later," he whispered back.

Laura stormed out of the shop, got in her car, and sped off. Being kicked out of the shop was unexpected, but she thought they could get an award for acting. Now she would have to work from home and frowned. She didn't want to be away from Axel.

Axel texted that he was on the way to Laura's condo. Laura had stopped at the grocery store for some steaks to cook on the condo's grills. She bought baked potatoes and a couple of cans of green beans.

She expected Axel to know how to grill the steaks. She'd googled how to bake the potatoes and would open the cans of beans.

When he arrived, she told him of her plans for that night's meal.

"Do you have any barbecue utensils?"

"No."

"Do you have any rubs to put on the steaks?"

"No."

"Princess, we might be going out to eat then."

Laura frowned. Axel showed up in his filthy jeans and stained shirt, which she'd seen him wear in the shop that morning.

"Well, not in those clothes we're not."

Axel looked down at his clothes. "Not fancy enough for you, Princess?"

"It's not that. It's just, well, some of the nicer steak restaurants have a dress code."

"I don't want to eat in any place that has a dress code."

Laura opened her mouth to argue but closed it without saying anything.

"Where can I get barbecue utensils and whatever else you said you need?"

"If you have a big fork or tongs, I can probably use those for tonight. Do you have any spices?"

"Spices? Like salt and pepper?"

Axel sighed. "Salt and pepper will have to do. Do you have butter?"

"Oh yes. I got that and sour cream for the baked potatoes."

"Did you put the potatoes in already?"

"Not yet."

"Princess, I'm going to have to send you to a cooking school. Those are going to take a while to bake. Put them in now and I'll get started on preparing the steaks. We might not be eating until midnight at this rate."

Laura's face fell in disappointment. She had wanted to do something nice for their meal.

"Listen, why don't I make a list of some spices you can get at the grocery store next time you go. Then you'll have them on hand. I really do like a good steak."

Laura's face brightened. "OK. That would be great."

Laura scrubbed the potatoes and put them in the oven. She waited to open the cans of green beans.

Axel rubbed butter over the steaks and put salt and pepper on them. "Have any garlic?" he asked.

Laura shook her head.

"Put that on your list."

He put the steaks on a plate and Laura showed him where the community grills were near the swimming pool. She stood with him while he started the gas grill and waited for the grill to heat up.

"How do you like your steak? Never mind. I'm cooking these steaks medium-rare. That's the best flavor."

"That's exactly how I like mine."

Axel put the steaks on the grill, turning them once, and then putting them back on the plate when they were done. He and Laura went back to her condo, where she started to heat the green beans. She checked on the potatoes, but they were far from being done.

"Might need to finish them off in the microwave," Axel said.

Laura took them out of the oven. "How long do you think?"

"Let's start with a couple of minutes. We don't want them too done."

"Won't the steaks get cold?"

"Turn the oven off and we'll put them in there to stay warm."

Laura felt like a fool for not knowing how to cook basic things. She was irritated that her mother hadn't really shown her how to cook. Her grandmother had always been the one to cook for the family.

After her grandmother died, Laura's mother Carmela cooked for the family, but Laura was a teenager by then and had no interest in learning from her. Laura just wanted to hang out with her friends, not be stuck in the kitchen with her mother bossing her around and telling her how to cook.

"I guess you can tell I'm not a great cook," Laura said when they were eating their steaks.

Axel laughed. "Princess, I knew you didn't cook the first time I looked in your refrigerator. It was empty."

"You seem to know how to cook. You could teach me."

"I know how to grill. That's pretty much it. My ex-wife used to do all the cooking and in prison, well, someone else did all the cooking. And I really wouldn't call that cooking. A lot of the prison meals we were served weren't fit for a dog."

Laura chewed her steak. "Well, this is excellent. Done just the way I like it."

Axel grinned. "What's for dessert?"

Now it was Laura's turn to grin at him. "You know what's for dessert."

The couple continued this routine for the next week. Laura would work from home, ensuring she touched base with her clients and her new intern.

Molly Sinclair reminded Laura a little of herself at that age. Molly was eager to learn and would help Laura with some of the posting to Star 1's accounts. It helped that she lived in the area and could go by the winery and take photos.

Laura had not met Molly in person yet. With Kyle's permission, she had reached out to Napa Valley College, a two-year college, and posted about the position. She'd gotten about 20 resumes and narrowed it down to five students.

She'd then called all of them and narrowed her list of candidates to two. She'd asked each to submit a proposal for a new social media campaign.

Molly had come up with the idea to partner with three other nearby wineries to do a passport-type event. Patrons would get a stamp on their passports for visiting the wineries, posting photos to each winery's social media accounts, and bringing a friend on a second visit.

Laura wished she had thought of that idea. Molly, a communications major, wanted to concentrate on the marketing aspect, as well, when she eventually went to get her degree at a larger college.

With the time difference, they agreed the training would be from one to three o'clock on Eastern time Monday, Tuesday, and Thursday.

Much of the training would be done via email and Slack.

On Friday, Laura decided to reach out to her mother to get some impromptu cooking lessons. She wanted to roast a chicken to show Axel she could do it.

"Laura!" her mother said with surprise when she called. "Is something the matter?"

"No, Mami. But I want to cook a nice meal for a friend, and I don't know how long to cook it. Can you tell me?"

"What kind of friend is this? A boyfriend?" Carmela asked.

"He's not a boyfriend, Mami. Just a friend."

"A friend you want to cook a special meal for? That sounds like a boyfriend to me," Carmela said.

Laura sighed. She did not want to have this conversation with her mother. She regretted calling, but then asked, "Can you help me, please?"

"Who is this friend? Does he have a nice family?"

"He's here in Atlanta by himself, so I want to cook him a nice meal, Mami. Please, no more questions!"

Carmela sighed into to the phone. "First, buy the freshest chicken you can. Do you have a market where you can get a live chicken?"

Laura frowned. There is no way I'm buying a live chicken, she thought. Laura was now considering getting a bucket of fried chicken from a fast-food place.

"No, Mami."

"Very well. Your grandmother will roll over in her grave, but you'll have to buy a frozen one. It won't be nearly as good," Carmela said with authority.

Laura realized her grandmother probably killed and plucked her own chickens back in Cuba, but Atlanta was not Cuba. Laura was not going near a live chicken.

"How big?"

"It's just the two of you for this date?"

"Yes, but I'll probably send him home with the leftovers. And it's not a date."

Carmela made a noise of derision. "Fine. Not a date. Get a five- to six-pound chicken. That should be plenty for two. Is he a big man?"

"He's pretty tall."

"But is he big? Like fat?"

"No, but he is pretty muscular. He works out a lot at the gym." And my bedroom, Laura thought, but didn't say.

"Make it an eight-pound chicken. He'll probably eat a lot."

"OK, so an eight-pound chicken. Now what?"

"Thaw it out in your refrigerator. Not on the counter, *mi hija*. You don't want to make him sick."

"Make him sick?" Laura said, now worried. If she made Axel puke, she'd never see him again.

"Just thaw it out in the refrigerator and you'll be fine."

"How many days?"

"Two should be plenty."

"Then what?"

"Do you have a roasting pan?"

"No."

"Laura!" Carmela said, exasperated with her daughter. "Buy a roasting pan. You need a roasting pan."

Laura felt near tears. She wanted to show Axel she could roast a chicken for him, and she realized she was ill-equipped to do so.

"I'll buy a pan today," she said, her voice cracking.

"Don't cry, *mi hija*. It will be fine. Do you have a pen? Write this down. Put your oven on 350 degrees and put the chicken in the roasting pan. Do you have some white wine?"

"Yes."

"And herbs?"

"I have salt and pepper, garlic. I had some herbs, but they went bad."

"Get some onions, too. Cut those up and put them in the pan with the chicken. And the garlic. Buy some dried rosemary and parsley. You can get them in the spice aisle, in bottles. Fresh is best, but you don't cook enough so dried will have to do. Put that on the chicken and salt and pepper. Then put some wine in the pan with the chicken."

"OK."

"Cook it for two hours."

"Two hours? Are you sure?"

"Who is the one asking for help? Of course, I'm sure!"

"I'm sorry, Mami. That just seems like a long time."

"For an eight-pound chicken, it should be fine."

"Thanks, Mami.

"I want to meet this man!"

"He's here in Atlanta. You are there in Miami. I doubt you will meet him."

"When you come home for Thanksgiving, bring him."

Laura rolled her eyes. "We'll see about Thanksgiving, Mami."

"You need to spend Thanksgiving with your family."

"*Sí*, Mami. I'll try to be there."

Laura was nervous as she puttered around her own kitchen Thursday evening. She'd purchased a roasting pan, a frozen eight-pound chicken, the herbs her mother had suggested, and some that Axel had told her to buy.

At her mother's suggestion, she bought fresh green beans, not those in a can, and fresh corn. Her mother told her to boil the corn and steam the green beans. That meant Laura had to buy a steamer as well.

She told Axel she had a surprise for him for Sunday dinner.

He arrived at her condo around eight o'clock Friday evening with his overnight bag and his dirty laundry. He got his laundry started and took a quick shower. Then he joined her in the kitchen.

"What's this big surprise on Sunday?"

"I'm making you dinner."

"You're making it? No takeout or delivery?"

"Nope."

"What is it?"

"I'm roasting a chicken. I'm making fresh corn and green beans, too."

"I'm impressed. Did you take a cooking course this past week I didn't know about?"

Laura made a face at Axel and playfully hit his muscular arm. "No. I called my mother and she told me what to do."

Axel raised his eyebrows. "Your mother?"

"Yes, my mother. I do talk to her every now and again."

"I'm not saying you don't. You just never talk about your parents. Other than you told me they live in Miami, and they used to be named Lopez, I don't know too much about them."

"I told you my grandparents came over from Cuba," she explained. "My father was a young boy. My mother's family was also from Cuba, but she was an infant when they came over."

Laura poured herself a glass of wine and offered one to Axel, who shook his head. He poured himself a cola, which Laura had also purchased at the grocery store.

"Both families were Catholic, and they met in school. Both sets of my grandparents lived within blocks of each other. We were definitely in a Cuban part of Miami. People called it Little Havana."

Axel shook his head. He was fascinated by her family story. It was so different from his.

"Anyway, they met and married. They moved into the Lopez house. It was very cramped when my brother and I lived there. My grandmother was still alive, but she lived in a small bedroom on the first floor. She couldn't get up and down the stairs that well. My parents converted that room to a kind of den after she died."

"And the family name was Lopez, not Lucas?"

"Correct. My abuelo wanted an American name. I guess he liked Lucas."

"Abuelo?"

"Grandfather."

"Did your mother's family change their last name, too?"

"No, and that caused a bit of a disagreement between the two families. My mother's maiden name is Perez. And believe me, the Perez family thought the Lopez family was a bit too uppity to take an American last name just to fit in. Like they were turning their backs on Cuba."

"I guess I can see their point."

"So can I, but it's what they did."

"Would you ever change your name back?"

"Oh, hell no. I've grown up my whole life as Laura Lucas."

"When are we having this delicious roasted chicken courtesy of your mother's instructions?"

"Sunday afternoon. I put the chicken in the refrigerator before you got here so it will be thawed out by Sunday afternoon."

The couple went out to dinner Saturday night at Buckhead Diner. Laura wore an emerald green wrap dress, along with her heels. Axel wore a new pair of khaki pants, a dress shirt and sports jacket.

"I didn't know you owned a sports jacket," Laura said, when he pulled it out of her closet.

"I didn't until this week, Princess. You can get some great shit at the Goodwill in Buckhead."

"I bet you can. Every woman in Buckhead clears out her ex-husband's closet after the divorce and his stuff ends up at Goodwill," Laura laughed, "or burning on the front lawn."

Axel snickered. "I'm thankful for the guy whose recent divorce means I can get a nice jacket for cheap."

Axel got the filet mignon and Laura opted for the pork chop. When they finished, Laura tried to slide her credit card over to Axel, but he pushed her hand away.

He took out a roll of twenties and paid the bill with cash.

When they got back to her car, Axel said, angry. "Don't ever do that again, Princess. I'm not your kept man."

"I'm sorry. I should have asked if you were paying tonight."

"Let's just be clear," he said, his voice low. "I can pay for a nice meal out every now and again. Maybe not a place this fancy every time. But I can pay."

"I'm sorry. I won't do it again."

"Good."

They were quiet on the ride back to Laura's condo, the mood inside the car turning sour.

When they got into the parking lot, the couple got out of the car and Axel said, "I think maybe I should go home tonight."

Laura couldn't keep the shock out of her face. "Axel Please don't go. I said I was sorry and I am. Please come upstairs."

"Do you understand how emasculating it is to have you try to pay for me?" he said, raising his voice. "Do you know how that makes me feel?"

"Please come upstairs. I don't want to argue in the parking deck."

Axel blew out a breath and opened the door to the lobby, striding over to the elevator and punching the up button. Laura came in behind him. They again didn't speak on the way up to her condo.

Laura opened her front door and Axel held it open while Laura entered.

"I'm sorry I yelled at you, but you have to understand how that makes me feel."

"I never meant to do that," Laura said, her voice cracking.

"Princess," Axel said, taking her hand. "You are a woman who always gets her way. I understand that. But you have to stop. I can't be a man who you pay for sex."

"That is not what I'm doing at all!" Laura exclaimed.

"Isn't it?"

"No!"

"I think we should agree who will pay when we go out for dinner before we even get in the car."

"OK. Whatever you want," Laura said, beginning to cry. "Just please don't leave me."

Axel pulled Laura to him into an embrace. "Oh, Princess. This is just our first real fight. That doesn't include all those other fights, I guess. Maybe this is our one hundredth fight."

Laura tried to laugh, but it came out choked. Axel rubbed her back. "Hush, Princess. It's going to be alright."

That seemed to make Laura cry harder. Axel looked into her face and wiped her tears.

"Please don't cry on this jacket," he said. "I just bought it."

Laura began to laugh through her tears.

Chapter 14

Laura woke in Axel's arms, the couple having made up before they went to bed that night. Laura now understood the appeal of makeup sex. She didn't enjoy the fight, but she did enjoy what came after.

The couple lingered in bed. Axel ran his finger over Laura's right nipple, then began to kiss and suck it. He then placed his hand on her other breast and began to knead it.

Laura arched her back and groaned. She reached down to feel for Axel's shaft, but he shifted away from her. "Let me just enjoy your body, Princess. Then you can enjoy mine," he whispered.

Axel began kissing down Laura's body, kissing her ribs, her stomach, and right above her pubic bone. He parted her labia and began to rub her clit. Then he gently blew on it.

Laura groaned again and arched her back. Axel finally began to suck her clit and flicked his tongue over it.

Laura balled her fists, grabbing her cotton sheets. The pleasure was so exquisite it was almost painful.

Axel then put his finger inside her and Laura began squeezing her vaginal walls around it.

"Princess, you are nice and wet," he whispered.

"Axel. Axel," she grunted. "Oh, God."

Axel raised himself over Laura and straddled her. Laura opened her eyes and opened her legs.

Axel lowered himself into her and began stroking inside her rhythmically. Laura began to pant with every stroke. So did Axel, his deep throaty grunt coming every time he pushed into her.

Laura held onto Axel's muscular arms, her breasts moving up and down with each stroke.

She felt her orgasm building, trying to hold it off for as long as she could. She began a long scream as she came. Axel then began his own deep guttural shout.

Laura could feel Axel's semen seeping out of her with every stroke.

"Oh, Princess. Princess," he said as he collapsed by her side. "Oh, God. I love you so much."

Laura curled toward him, wrapping her left leg over his body to try to get closer to him. "I love you, too," she whispered.

Axel was surprised. He thought he'd be declaring his love without a response. He didn't expect her to tell him she loved him.

"How do you know?" he asked simply.

Laura started to cry. "I don't know," she croaked. "I just know that I do. I love you so much."

"Hush, Princess. It's alright. I love you, too."

They awoke much later that morning. Laura felt embarrassed by her declaration of love. She hadn't said she'd loved any man since Julio. She wasn't used to being in love again. She felt frightened by her revelation.

Axel stirred and rolled over to face her. "I love you, Princess. Did you hear me? I love you."

"I heard you."

"You said you loved me back."

Laura sighed. "I know. It scares me."

"Why?"

Laura looked away and took a deep breath. "The last man I said I loved was Julio."

Axel's face darkened. "Princess, I'm not going to beat or rape you."

Axel got up on one elbow and turned Laura's face to his. He looked her in the eyes. "That man did not love you. If he had, he'd never have treated you that way. Never. That's not love."

"I know that now. Because your love feels easy. I feel free."

"Have you had any more dreams of him?"

Laura thought about it. The realization surprised her. "Not since I started sleeping with you. You exorcized my ghost."

Laura wrapped her arms around Axel and pulled him into her. "Oh, God, I love you, Axel. I love you." Laura wanted to shout it from her condo balcony. She loved this man.

They finally got out of bed, lazily. Laura suggested they shower together. "To save water," Laura joked.

They soaped each other's bodies. Axel enjoyed washing Laura's hair, taking deep fistfuls in his hands, and soaping it up.

"I know you shave your head. What color was your hair?" Laura asked.

"It was brown. It still is brown. I guess I could grow it out again. I've just kept it shaved ever since prison."

Laura's eyes widened. "Would you? Would you grow it out for me? I'd like to see it. I'd like to run my fingers through it."

Axel thought for a moment in the steamy shower. "Sure, Princess. I'll regrow it. But if I want to shave it all off again, I can. You have no say in it."

"OK. You are right. It's your hair, or lack of it."

"Promise me, Princess. I decide if I want to shave it off again."

"I promise."

They toweled each other off, with Laura wrapping her hair in a plush white towel.

"I should get our dinner started," Laura said, putting on an oversized designer top and leggings. Axel put on some sweatpants and a white tank.

"I'm looking forward to this dinner," he said, wrapping his arms around her waist as she stood in front of the refrigerator. She pulled out the chicken and put it on the counter.

She brushed off Axel's arms and reached for her new roaster. She followed her mother's instructions and chopped some a yellow onion and two cloves of garlic. She was careful not to cut her manicured nails.

She buttered the chicken, added salt and pepper, and put dried rosemary and parsley all over the chicken as well.

She opened a bottle of white wine. When she placed everything in the roaster, she pulled out the wine. Then she looked at Axel.

"Oh. My mother said to add wine. Can I add it? Would you rather I not? I know you are sober."

"I think the oven will burn off all the alcohol, Princess. Go ahead and add it."

"Thanks." She poured half the bottle of white wine into the roaster.

Two hours later, Laura was triumphantly taking the roaster out of the oven. As her mother had suggested, she left the chicken to rest on the counter.

The corn and beans she prepared just before the chicken was out of the oven. She'd added a little salt to the water, as her mother had also instructed, for the corn and steamed the green beans, carefully cutting off the stems before she did so.

When it was all out on the table, she'd buttered the corn and beans.

As she started to cut the chicken, Laura realized the chicken was not quite done. Her mother had instructed her to check the chicken. If the juices ran clear, or white, it was done. If they ran pink, it wasn't done.

Laura's chicken ran pink as she cut into it. Then she realized there was an organ package in the cavity. She'd never taken it out. She never knew it was there.

She grabbed Axel's plate. "I'm sorry. I don't think this is quite right. We better microwave this."

Axel burst out laughing. "Oh, Princess."

Laura felt a tear slip down her cheek. "I wanted this to be perfect for you."

"It is perfect. It's just your first time roasting a chicken. I bet the next time you get it exactly right."

They put their chicken in the microwave and then put the corn and beans on their plates.

When they finally sat down to eat it was later than expected. Axel kept reassuring Laura the meal was delicious.

"But I messed up," Laura lamented. "I ruined the meal. I don't want to make you sick. My God, you'll break up with me on the spot!"

"You did fine. I enjoyed this," he said, pushing his empty plate away from him.

"I was hoping to send you home with the leftovers, but I'm not sure. I think we'll have to throw the chicken out."

"I'm sorry I won't get the rest of this."

"You can take the corn and the beans home," Laura said, looking hopeful. "Maybe we can microwave the rest of the chicken."

"I'll take whatever you give me, Princess."

When Axel finally left Laura's condo, Laura held Axel close.

"I hate to see you go," she said. "I love you. More than I've loved anyone."

"And I love you, Princess. I don't want to think of my life without you."

Once the couple had declared their love for one another, they found it impossible to stay apart. That created an unexpected problem.

Axel's parole officer came by the shop one Friday evening to check on him, and Axel was not there. Axel was already at Laura's place.

The text message that Axel received, shocked him. He knew the parole officer could make an unannounced visit, but in his love and need for Laura, he'd forgotten. Axel quickly texted he was in Buckhead and gave the address.

The parole officer arrived an hour later. Laura and Axel found themselves in an awkward position. Axel had to give Laura's address as an alternative address for his location. Axel hoped Kye didn't find out.

The parole officer's visit unnerved them both.

"I'm sorry I had to give him your address," Axel said. "I didn't want to get you involved in this."

"If it involves you, it involves me," she said.

"If the parole officer can't find me, it's a violation of my parole."

"Then he needs this address."

"I'm going to make a suggestion you won't like."

Axel could see a look of concern on Laura's face.

"Are you breaking up with me?" she asked, feeling like she might cry.

"No, Princess. Not that," he said, going in to hug her. "I don't think I should spend every night at your place. I think we should come up with a schedule, so I'll be at the shop when the parole officer calls or visits."

"But he can just check on you here," she said.

"He can, but this place is way too fancy. He might accuse me of getting together with you for the wrong reasons."

"What reasons?"

"Your money."

"My money?"

Axel looked around Laura's condo. "Let's face it. You live far better than I can afford. You have nice clothes, nice jewelry, nice everything." Axel waved his hand around the condo.

That made Laura angry. "Are you saying you are only with me for my money? Because if that were the case, I'd be buying dinner more often."

"Now don't get all bent, Princess. That is not why I'm with you and why I don't want you to pay for our dinners out."

"Then why can't you just have the parole officer find you here?"

"I wish I could make you understand it might look bad for me."

"You don't want to come over here anymore?" Laura asked, exasperated. "Because I really don't want to stay over at the shop."

"That's not what I said. And I wouldn't expect you to stay over at the shop, Princess. Let's just work out a schedule so I'm not staying over as much."

"I don't like that idea," Laura pouted. "I want to be with you."

"I have to say I'm flattered considering you couldn't stand the sight of me when we met," Axel laughed.

"That was then," said Laura, not smiling. She didn't find what Axel said funny. "Before I got to know you."

"Listen, Princess," Axel said, more serious now. "This isn't forever. I'm not going to be on parole forever. I just think for right now, I have to be careful. I can't do anything to make my parole officer decide I've violated parole. That's why I don't drink."

"What do you mean?"

"If my parole officer shows up and I've been drinking, or worse yet, drunk, that could violate my parole."

"I didn't know that. Does it bother you that I drink?"

"It bothers me that you think you need to drink. You could enjoy a meal without a glass of wine."

"Oh no I couldn't," Laura said in all earnestness.

"Yes, you could, Princess. You just don't want to."

"You are right. I don't want to. I enjoy a glass of wine with my meals."

"I'm not judging you."

"Feels like you are," Laura snapped, crossing her arms across her chest.

"Princess, I don't want to fight again. Please, let's just work out a schedule where I'm back at the shop a few nights a week and not here. Do this for me."

"OK," she said, quietly. "I don't like it, but I'll do it for you."

"Thank you," he said, pulling her into an embrace.

The couple spent that night together but agreed — Laura rather reluctantly — that Axel would only stay over every other night, except on the weekends.

Laura didn't like the thought of Axel sleeping alone at the shop. She insisted he call her before he went to bed, and they ended up talking for hours.

"Princess, you are going to have to hang up. I need to sleep. It's a busy day tomorrow."

"Very well. Good night."

"Good night, Princess. I love you."

"I love you, too."

Axel didn't give Laura a chance to keep the conversation going. He hung up on her.

Chapter 15

By mid-August, the couple had made their new routine a habit. Axel's parole officer hadn't visited since that time Axel was not at the shop, but he still checked in on the parolee every week. Axel had to report to the parole officer and respond to texts and phone calls.

Axel found he enjoyed his nights at the shop. He'd begun to read his books again and went to the gym regularly. At Laura's condo, he'd go down to the fitness center, but that didn't have all the equipment of his gym.

Axel had set some ground rules, however. Laura could only call once in the evening when he was at the shop.

"Once a night?" Laura complained.

"Princess, you know I love you, but I need some downtime too."

"Have your downtime at my place."

Axel laughed. "Then it wouldn't be downtime. I'll see you tomorrow after work."

"I'd think you got enough downtime at work," she grumbled.

"You do realize how busy the shop has become. There is no downtime when I'm working on cars or helping techs. And if we go ahead with the second shop, I'll be even busier. So will you."

Laura frowned. She didn't want to spend less time with Axel. She wanted to spend more time with him. She wanted him all to herself.

"Well, I'm not happy," was all she could say.

"Sorry, Princess. I'll see you tomorrow after work."

The next morning, Laura paced in her condo. She was having trouble concentrating. She needed to write some press releases for Buon Cibo and Star 1. But she ended up sitting down at her laptop, then getting up and pacing her condo again. She wasn't sure why she was so antsy and anxious.

She wanted to call Axel. But she promised herself, and him, that she would only call him once in the evening.

Laura sat back down at her laptop. She stared at it, unable to concentrate. She pushed her laptop across the table.

Maybe if she distracted herself, ideas would come to her. But how?

If she couldn't talk to Axel, who could she talk to? Laura picked up her cellphone and dialed her parent's number in Miami.

Her mother Carmela answered after the third ring, breathless. Laura could imagine her mother quickly coming down the stairs to answer the landline phone in the kitchen. She wished they'd let her buy them a cellphone.

"Hello?" her mother asked.

"Mami! It's me. How are you and Papi?"

"Laura? What is the matter? Are you sick?"

"No, Mami. I just wanted to call to see how you are."

"We are fine. And how are you?"

"I am fine. I've been busy with work."

"Well, I don't want to keep you."

"Oh. Well, alright. You give Papi a kiss from me."

"Laura, are you sure you are alright?"

"I'm fine. Just missing you both."

"We miss you too. Come visit us."

"I'll look at my calendar, Mami. Love to you and Papi."

Laura hung up. She almost regretted calling her mother, except she suddenly missed them both. She felt sure her mother was confused as to why she had called. Laura rarely called her parents out of the blue.

She still wanted to chat with someone. Laura had an epiphany. She'd call Guillerma.

Laura dialed her cell number and Guillerma picked up on the second ring.

"Hi, Laura, what's up?" Guillerma asked.

"Oh, I was just calling to see how you are. Are you at work? Am I disturbing you?"

"I'm at work, but I can talk for a minute. When are you coming to Miami?"

"My mother asked the same thing. I've got to look at my calendar."

"Well, when you come, we'll have to go shopping again."

"I'd love that. I love that new Hermes bag I got."

"Well, it's been almost a year. You need a new one!"

Laura laughed. "I sure do."

"Come soon and we'll go to some of the clubs."

"Do you still go to the clubs?"

"Hell yes, *amiga*! Sometimes I go with my girlfriends. I make Benny watch the kids. I need a night out on the town!"

Benny was Guillerma's husband. Laura couldn't imagine him letting her go out to the clubs with her girlfriends. Maybe he's a modern man, she thought.

"If I get down there soon, I'll have to go with you."

"That would be fun. Oh, they are calling me. I've got to go back to work. Thanks for calling. Bye."

Before Laura could tell Guillerma goodbye, her friend had hung up.

Laura smiled. She could see her and Guillerma becoming friends, going to clubs together, gossiping over mojitos. Laura now longed to fly down to Miami and have some fun.

She opened her laptop now and looked at flights to her childhood home. Maybe she could swing a short trip. Before she could think about it, she'd booked a flight at the end of September.

She'd call her mother and Guillerma to let them know of her plans. She hoped they wouldn't have plans. Maybe she should have consulted them first.

Laura shook her head. Her parents never went anywhere, and it sounded like Guillerma stayed close to home, too.

She brightened and her mood lifted. She was looking forward to being in Miami.

Laura then shook her head. She hadn't even thought about Axel. She hadn't consulted with him or asked him. Surely, he'd be alright with her trip to see her parents. She'd tell him about it when she talked to him that night.

"I think it's great you are going to see your parents, Princess. I don't mind."

"I was worried since I didn't ask you first."

"You don't have to ask me. But I will miss you while you are gone."

"I'll miss you, too." Laura hesitated a moment. "Can I come to your place tonight?"

"You want to come here? To the shop?"

"I want to be with you, Axel. I won't stay all night if you are worried about that."

"Princess, we talked about this."

"I know we did. But I want to see you tonight. I won't stay all night. I promise. Can I come to the shop? I'll get some take out. Do you like Indian food? There's a great Indian restaurant near me."

"Do you like Thai food? There's a good Thai place just down from me."

"I love Thai food."

Laura gave Axel a list of some of her favorite Thai dishes. Axel said he'd pick up some food after the shop closed and he'd see her later that evening.

Laura got to the shop shortly before eight. Axel's truck was parked near the side door, so she knew he was back from getting their dinner. She knocked on the door.

Axel let her in. Laura could see some tea lights lit on the receptionist's counter.

"When did you get these?" Laura asked in wonder.

"I got them at Target one time on my way home from your place. I've used them a couple of times when the power has gone out. I put them to better use tonight, Princess."

Laura could feel tears in her eyes. The shop looked beautiful in the tea light glow. She could smell the food and felt pangs of hunger.

"I got a couple of dishes you said you liked."

"Did you get something you like?"

"Of course, I did. I go to Saigon Basil a lot. I've got several favorites."

They sat in the shop's break room and ate their dinner.

"Sorry, Princess. I didn't get you any wine."

Axel pulled out a 2-liter bottle of cola and a smaller bottle of water.

"I'm fine with water tonight."

Axel quickly prayed before he ate. Laura sat opposite him in silence. Praying just wasn't her thing.

When they finished their meal, Axel packed up the takeout boxes and put them in his mini fridge in his office. He'd have the leftovers for lunch tomorrow.

They cuddled on the shop's small sofa, listening to music on Laura's iPhone.

After about an hour, Laura suggested they head to his office.

Axel inflated his full-sized air mattress, then put on sheets. Axel could almost feel Laura's nervous energy. He knew what she was anxious for.

She sat on the air mattress and bounced a few times. "This is almost like a water mattress."

"Except there's no water," Axel said.

"I wish we were at my place."

"Why? Don't you like making love under fluorescent lights?"

Laura laughed. "It certainly isn't flattering light. At my place, we have a real bed."

"Hey, I can make you appreciate a blow-up mattress."

"I doubt it."

"I'll make you eat those words."

Laura giggled. "Just you try. Come here," Laura said, laying back on the mattress. "I'm ready to bounce."

"Your wish is my command, Princess."

As the couple lay naked on the air mattress in the comfortable afterglow of their love making, they both drifted off to sleep.

Late in the night, Axel suddenly awoke after hearing glass breaking in the shop.

Instinctively, he reached under the mattress for his gun and sat up. The gun wasn't there. He'd left it in his office desk when he and Laura had made love.

He reached over and opened the drawer to get it, feeling its weight in his hand.

Laura was slower to awake and sat up to see Axel at the doorway of the office.

"Stay in the office. Lock the door."

He left the office and went out the shop's bay door to check on the sounds he heard.

Laura suddenly heard gunfire and screamed. She shot out of the office screaming, "Axel! Axel!"

She found the side door open and ran outside, naked.

"Get back inside, Laura," Axel commanded.

"I heard gunshots! Oh, Axel!" She started crying, afraid for him.

"Get inside," he said, grabbing her by the arm and forcing her through the side door.

Laura stood in the dark, shivering with fear.

Axel finally came back into the shop, gun still in his hand.

"I had to pick up the shells. I shot at the burglar. I didn't hit him. I shot high. But I can't have the shells in the parking lot. I'm sure the police are going to come. Get dressed. We're going back to your place. "

Laura stood stock still, paralyzed with fear.

"Now!" Axel shouted.

Laura still didn't move. Axel dragged her by the arm into the office. "Get dressed, Laura. Please. I can't have the police searching this office and finding this gun," he said, showing her the weapon.

Laura got dressed. Axel tucked the gun in his waistband. He then went inside his office and erased the tape from the security cameras, although the tape was so grainy no one would likely be able to see faces.

"Are you OK to drive?"

Laura nodded.

"Drive home. I'll follow you."

Laura climbed into her car, still shaking with fear. She drove home, seemingly on autopilot, not really paying attention to the road.

Thankfully, she and Axel arrived at her condo unharmed. They clung to each other in the elevator on the way up to her penthouse.

Laura could not stop shaking. She felt so cold. Axel held her tight until they got to her door.

Laura had trouble opening the door and then resetting her security system.

"I feel like I'm back in prison," Axel said, as she finally set the alarm.

That stunned Laura. "Why would you say that?"

"All this extra security. You can't tell me you honestly need this."

"I do need it!" she shouted. "I need to keep Julio from coming in!"

"Julio is dead!"

"He still haunts me," Laura said, her voice breaking.

"Still? You said you weren't having any more nightmares about him."

"I don't have many anymore. Not since I've been with you. But I'm always afraid I will again."

"Oh, Princess," Axel said, holding her in a tight embrace. "I'm sorry he hurt you. I'm sorry you still have dreams of him."

"I don't want to dream of him anymore," Laura cried. "I don't want to think of him anymore. Hold me tighter."

Axel held her, stroking her hair while she sobbed.

Chapter 16

Laura and Axel did not make love at her place. Instead, they held each other in bed for most of the night, unable to sleep.

Laura finally got up and opened a bottle of the Star 1 Cabernet and poured a large glass. She drank it in three gulps, then poured another.

Axel got up and followed her into the kitchen. "Are you just going to get drunk tonight?"

"Maybe."

"Then I'm going back to the shop," Axel said.

"Why?"

"Princess, I think you drink to hide your pain."

"When did you become Dr. Lynch?" Laura sneered.

"Don't get mad at me. I just think you drink to stop feeling your pain."

"Maybe I do. I have a lot of pain, Axel!" she shouted, then started sobbing again. She threw the nearly full glass of wine across her kitchen. The wine glass shattered as it hit the tile floor.

Laura sank to the ground and lay flat on the floor.

"Get up," Axel told her, nudging her with his foot.

"Why are you being so mean?"

"I'm not being mean. I want you to get up and come back to bed."

"And what? Do you want to have sex now?"

"No. I want you to come back to bed and get some sleep. You need some sleep. Hell, I need some sleep. I've got to work tomorrow."

"And I don't?" Laura shouted. "I've got work tomorrow too!"

"Then come to bed," he said, holding out his hand to her. Laura let him help her off the kitchen floor.

When they got back in bed, Axel said, "I tell you one thing. I'm telling Kyle to get better security for the shop. You could have been hurt."

Axel's voice broke. "If anything had happened to you . . ."

Laura held Axel as close as she could, and he held her right back. They finally fell asleep clutching each other.

Axel called Kyle the next morning, altering the details of the break-in. He did not tell Kyle that Laura was with him. He'd said he was alone when the break-in attempt had occurred. He also did not say why he didn't call the police. He'd call the police later to report the broken window for the insurance paperwork.

Axel demanded Kyle add extra security to the shop. He wanted better cameras. He explained the ones he had produced pictures so grainy as to be worthless.

"What's it going to take, Kyle?" Axel demanded. "When you are attending my funeral?"

"Fine. Get the security system you want. I'll ask Laura to find the best one. I'll take care of it."

"You better."

Kyle next called Laura to tell her to call companies and price a better security system for Axel's Motors.

Laura almost blurted out that she'd been at the shop when it was broken into, but at the last moment, she caught herself. "I'll be happy to do that. I'll have to go down to the shop, I suppose. You know Axel kicked me out of the shop, don't you?"

"I heard that."

Laura then knew Axel was correct when he suspected there was a spy at the shop. There's no way Kyle would have known that unless someone at the shop had told him.

"I'll call Axel and see if he will let me back in the shop to talk to him about his needs."

"You do that." Kyle then hung up.

Despite being told not to call Axel at the shop, she did.

"Step into your office," she told him when he answered his cellphone.

"What's up?" Axel said as he closed his office door.

"You were right about a spy. Kyle knew about our shouting match when you kicked me out of the shop and told me not to return. You didn't tell him about that, did you?"

"Nope."

"He knew. So, you have a spy in your office."

"I suspected. Now I know. We have to be even more careful. No more coming to my office for dinner or anything else."

"Jesus Christ don't worry. I won't. I don't want to get shot."

"I don't want anything to happen to you, either. God, if anything had happened to you."

"Axel. It didn't. We'll be extra careful now. I see that we need to be careful."

"I wish we could just tell him."

"Don't. For sure he'd fire me. He told me explicitly that I'm not to sleep with another one of his employees."

"I hate to ask this, but how many of his employees have you slept with?"

"One."

"Just one?"

"Well, maybe two, but one was an employee, and one was a partner."

"Oh, that makes me feel a whole lot better," Axel said with sarcasm. "A partner. That doesn't count."

"Axel, I'm sorry. I know I have a somewhat checkered past. I've slept with a lot of men. But I don't want to do that any more. I only want you. I love you."

Axel said nothing.

"Are you angry with me?"

"I'm not happy."

"Please. Let's talk about this at my place tonight. Please come to my place tonight."

Axel still said nothing. Laura could cry at the silence.

"Please," she whispered.

"I'll be there after work."

Axel drove aggressively to Laura's house. He was angry at her and himself that it mattered to him how many men she had slept with.

He knew she wasn't a virgin. He didn't expect her to be a virgin. She said she'd been raped as a teen. But it unsettled him to think that she'd slept with two of Kyle's employees. And now she was sleeping with him.

Was this just a game to her? How many of Kyle's lackeys had she slept with? Was he just another notch on her bedpost?

He arrived at her parking garage angry. He ignored the concierge as he said "Hello, Mr. Lynch. So nice to see you this evening," and pushed the elevator door to take him to the penthouse.

Axel pounded on Laura's front door.

When she opened it, he rushed in, not even greeting her with a kiss.

"We need to get this out in the open," he said, his fists balled up by his side. "I don't want a detailed list but ballpark it for me. How many men have you slept with?"

Laura's jaw dropped and her mind whirled. She had no idea how many men she'd slept with over the years.

"I, I, I," she stammered.

"You have no idea, do you?" he spat, pointing at her.

"No, I don't," she whispered, turning away from him.

"Dammit! I wish it didn't bother me, but it does." Axel ran his hand over the top of his head, now sporting the start of some brown hair. "I mean, I know you aren't a virgin. I don't expect you to be one. It's just," he sighed. "I guess I'm jealous of all those other men that had you before me."

"I'm sorry," she said, a tear rolling down her cheek. "None of those other men ever had my heart and soul, Axel. None of them. You do."

Axel blew out a long breath. "I'm sorry I yelled at you. I didn't come here to fight with you. Come here," he said, opening his arms.

Laura fell into his embrace. She hugged him hard.

"I wish I could take it all back," she cried. "I would if I could."

"Don't cry. I'm sorry I yelled. I never want to make you cry."

Laura wiped her eyes on Axel's T-shirt. Her black mascara left a smear on it.

"Thanks," he said, looking down at it. "Wasn't my favorite anyway."

"I'm sorry. Take it off and we'll wash it right now."

"Are you sure you're just not trying to get me out of my clothes?" he joked.

"Well, that's not a bad idea. I hear makeup sex can be incredibly satisfying."

Axel quickly took his shirt off and handed it to her. "But not before putting this in your washer."

After they made love, Laura whispered, "I was jealous of that woman, too."

"What woman?" Axel asked.

"The woman you made love to when you got out of prison. I wish it had been me."

Axel rolled over to face her. "I have a confession to make."

"Confession? You aren't Catholic."

"No, but I lied to you. You were the first woman I made love to out of prison."

Laura could feel the tears forming. "I'm so glad," she croaked.

"Now don't get all weepy on me again," he said, using his thumb to wipe her eyes.

"I want to ask you something. It's something we'd do together," Axel continued.

Laura looked alarmed. Was he going to ask her to marry him?

Axel could see the look on Laura's face. "I want us to start going to church together."

Laura's eyes got wide. "Why the hell would we do that?"

"I think it's important for both of us, Princess. I've been thinking about it a lot. I want to start going again. I haven't been since I was in prison."

"You went to church in prison?"

"We had a non-denominational service every Sunday. But I could go with you to the Catholic church."

"Well, you could, but I never go."

"Let's go together."

Laura looked at Axel skeptically. "Why do you really want to go?"

Axel sighed. "I found comfort in it – the service I mean. We had a good preacher. He came every week to the prison."

"And why do you want me to go?"

"I think we both need some grace and forgiveness, by God and for ourselves. Please, Princess. Come with me."

"You know Catholics don't always go on Sundays. Some go Saturday night."

Surprised, Axel asked, "Did your family ever do that?"

"Oh hell no. My mother and grandmother were Sunday service women. They wanted to be seen in church and all the good Catholics went on Sunday."

"Then we'll go on Sunday too."

Flustered, Laura let out a breath. "But I don't want to go anymore. I'm done with religion."

"Please go with me. Even if it's just once. I won't know how to do the stuff in Catholic church. You will."

"If I go once with you, I don't ever have to go again?"

"I'd hope you would like to go with me again and again. But if you don't want to go after the one time, I'll just have to find another church to go to. I want to go. I'm willing to go to a Catholic church, but without you, I'll go elsewhere."

Laura thought about it for a long minute. "I'll go with you, just once."

Axel sighed in relief. "Great. Where's the nearest Catholic church?"

"The one closest to my place is probably the Cathedral of Christ the King."

"We'll go on Sunday. What time is the service?"

"You mean this Sunday?"

"Why not? No time like the present."

"But I want to sleep in!"

"Not this Sunday."

Laura pouted. "I'll look up the times. Maybe they have a later mass."

Axel pulled Laura close and kissed her. "Thank you."

"I must really love you to do this."

"That's good to know."

"I might have to find a dress to wear."

"You have tons of dresses! I've seen your closet."

"Ah, those might be a little too revealing for church."

"Oh, I guess I might need something nicer than my jeans, too. Let's shop tomorrow. You can help me pick out something appropriate. Otherwise, I'll have to go to the Buckhead Goodwill and hope someone my size just got divorced."

Laura laughed, then turned serious. "I don't think you ll need a suit, but I'm looking forward to seeing you in a sports jacke I know you have the one, but you need more than one."

"Whatever you say, Princess."

Axel and Laura greeted the priest at the door at the end of mass. They introduced themselves when he said he did not re ognize them as members of the congregation.

"I certainly hope we will see more of you," he said.

Laura made a noncommittal comment, but Axel s id they'd be back next Sunday.

"Why did you say that?" she hissed as they finished e iting the gray stone church. "I will not be back next Sunday. I told you I'd go today but I did not say I would make this a regular event."

Axel reached for Laura's hand as she tried to storm t ward her car in the church's parking lot.

"Hold on," he said. "Don't be mad. I just saw the wa y you relaxed about halfway through the mass. You knew the respon es. I was the one who was completely lost. Thanks for letting me now when I needed to stand and all that."

Laura knew Axel was right. She was tense when the first arrived, but a few minutes into the mass, the familiar words a d responses made her relax. It was all so familiar, even though the m ass wasn't in Spanish.

Although she had seen a Hispanic woman down the row, and she was clearly saying the responses in Spanish. Laura caught erself saying a response in Spanish as well.

She was glad they hadn't really dressed up. Some of he men had golf shirts on and the women wore sundresses. Her gran mother must be rolling over in her grave.

Laura had purchased a navy short-sleeved dress tha came down just below her knees. She paired it with a light black sw ater and her Jimmy Choo sling-back sandals.

She'd found a pair of khaki pants for Axel and a light blue short-sleeved shirt, but he wore a navy sports jacket almost the same color as her dress. She was grateful the jacket covered his tattoos.

There was nothing to be done about the prison tattoos on his fingers, but at least they were a faded blue.

"Well, I don't know that I'll be back next week," she replied. "I just don't want you to say I will."

"Oh, you'll be back, and we both know it. Now let's be like all these other churchgoers and go out for lunch," he said.

"That's the best suggestion you've had all day. Is it OK if we go to a fancier place? I'll pay."

Axel smiled. "Yes. Since you came with me to church, you can pay for my lunch this time."

Laura smiled. "I know just the place."

They had to wait for a table at Bistro Niko, but Laura didn't mind. They sat at the bar. Axel had his cola and Laura had a glass of white wine.

"Damn, I'm glad you are paying," Axel said as he looked over the brunch menu. I'm getting the steak."

"I'm getting the eggs Benedict," she said as the waiter took their order. She also ordered another glass of wine. Axel raised an eyebrow. "Don't worry, I won't order another one."

"Good. I like your car, but I don't like driving it."

"Why not?"

"You have the seat up way too high and too close to the steering wheel."

"It's because I'm short, in case you haven't noticed."

"Oh, I've noticed, Princess."

"You can always change the seat, Axel."

"I'd rather not. It is set for you. It's your car."

"Well, I wouldn't like driving your truck either."

"You probably couldn't see over the steering wheel," Axel said with a guffaw.

Laura frowned. "Probably not. It's a good thing we each have our own cars."

"I like that dress on you. You were the prettiest one in church today."

"You're just saying that, so I'll go back."

"No, I mean it. You looked really nice. Thanks for going with me."

"You looked pretty handsome yourself. You look nice in a jacket. It matched my dress if you didn't notice."

"I did notice. We made a nice couple."

"I told you I'm going to Miami at the end of September," Laura said, changing the subject. "I can give you my key if you want to do your laundry at my place while I'm gone."

"That's fine, Princess. I can slum it down at the laundromat. How long will you be gone? A week?"

"No, just a few days."

"Will you go to church when you are there?"

"My mother will insist."

"I like your mother."

"She's not fond of you."

"How does she know? She's never met me. I am very charming," he said, giving Laura a big grin.

"I might have told her about your, umm, recent past before I got to know you."

"You told her I was a convicted felon," Axel said, now irritated with Laura.

"I'm sorry. It was before I got to know you. My parents were worried and didn't want me to be alone with you."

"You bad-mouthed me to *both* of your parents?"

"Listen, when I get there, I'll tell them how wonderful you are. How you've really helped me and how fond I am of you now."

Axel rolled his eyes. "Oh, that will make everything better," he said with sarcasm. "A real ringing endorsement from you."

"I said I was sorry. I didn't like you when I met you."

"The feeling was mutual, Princess."

"Please let's not argue here."

"Are you finished?"

Laura looked down at her meal, but she'd lost her appetite. "I guess so. I'm not hungry anymore."

"Neither am I."

Axel signaled for the waiter.

"May I box these up for you?"

"Sure," Axel said. "No sense in wasting a good steak."

Laura shook her head. She didn't want to keep half-eaten eggs Benedict.

Chapter 17

The couple drove back to Laura's condo in silence. When she parked her car next to Axel's truck he said, "I think I'll head back to the shop. I'll just get my things."

"No," Laura said, putting her hand on Axel's leg to keep him from getting out of the car. "Please don't go. I said I was sorry about telling my parents about you but that was before I got to know you."

Axel took his takeout box and got out of the car. "You know what? I'll come back for my stuff." Axel got in his truck and left Laura's parking garage.

Stunned, Laura returned to her condo and sobbed when she got through the door.

Axel drove back to the shop in a foul mood, angry with Laura and angry with himself. He'd prided himself in not caring what others thought of his past. But finding out Laura had told her parents about him, and that they didn't approve, made him feel ashamed.

He knew he should turn around and go back to Laura's condo and make up with her. He hadn't expected to be alone on a Sunday afternoon. He didn't want to be alone in the shop.

Axel decided to change out of his Sunday clothes and go to the gym. If he lifted weights and ran hard on the treadmill maybe he could forget his anger and shame.

Back at her condo, Laura changed out of her dress, took off her makeup, and began doing the rest of Axel's laundry, even folding it neatly as it came out of the dryer. She stacked the newly clean clothes in his laundry basket.

She considered bringing it to the shop. She doubted he had any towels or work clothes for the next day.

Laura didn't want to change into something nicer, so she took one of Axel's shirts and a pair of his gym shorts out of the basket. She'd have to wash them for him again when she got home.

Late that afternoon, she drove toward the shop, but when she pulled into the parking lot, she didn't see his truck. Where was he? She wondered. Should she leave his laundry basket by the side door? She had visions of some homeless people helping themselves to Axel's things.

Laura texted Axel. **I'm at the shop. I have your clean clothes. Where are you? Should I leave them by the side door?**

I'm at the gym. I'll be there in five. Don't leave.

Laura was nervous waiting for Axel. Maybe she should leave. He said he was coming back, so she could just leave his stuff and go.

Laura placed the laundry basket in front of the side door and had just gotten in her car when Axel's truck pulled into the parking lot. He parked right behind her, blocking her in.

He got out of his truck and rushed over to her driver's door, opening it. "I told you not to leave," he said, with more anger than he intended. He reached in and helped Laura out of the car.

"I just... I'm sorry," she said, bursting into tears once more.

Axel pulled her to him, stroking her hair. "I'm sorry, too. Come inside, please. Let's just talk."

Axel unlocked the side door and kicked the laundry basket inside, then led Laura back to his office.

"Sit in the chair," he told her.

Laura sat in his office chair and Axel went out to get a folding chair from the lobby. He set it up right across from her, so he could look at her.

"I'm sorry I was so angry with you, Princess. But you made me feel ashamed."

Laura looked up, wiping her eyes. "Ashamed? I didn't mean..."

"I know you didn't," he said, standing up and pacing before her. "I've never been ashamed of my past. But hearing you told your parents about me, and they didn't approve..."

Axel drew his hand through his now short-cropped hair. "I don't even know them and having them disapprove of me, well, it made me ashamed of who I am."

"Axel, I never want you to feel that way," she said, tears running down her cheeks. "You are a good man." She began sobbing again, burying her face in her hands.

Axel gave her a wan smile. "Never thought I'd hear you say that, Princess."

"But you are! You are caring and kind," she said between gulps of air.

"Hush, please don't cry," he said, pulling her to her feet. He then cupped her face in his hands and used his thumbs to wipe her tears away. They held each other tightly, then Laura asked, "Do you want to go back to my place?"

"I think I'll go ahead and stay here tonight, since it will be an early day. I've got a guy coming in at six to drop his car off so I can fix it the same day."

"Well, I can stay here," she said.

"You could, but it might not be safe."

"Didn't you get the new security?"

"I did, but I still don't think you should be here. You can't be seen leaving the shop if the techs are here, and a couple of them will be here early to help me with that car."

"Kyle and his spies," Laura spat.

Axel stroked Laura's hair as he held her again. "I really don't want you to leave," he whispered.

"I don't want to leave, either."

"Let's order takeout and have dinner here, at least. There's that Thai restaurant near here. Do you mind Thai food? I know we got it the last time."

"I love it. The spicier the better. Have them give us some of the garlic chili oil on the side."

"I have a paper menu in the drawer behind you. Let's decide what we want."

They ordered a couple of orders of spring rolls, a spicy beef dish and a spicy Thai eggplant dish with chicken.

They went to pick up their order, but Laura realized she'd have no wine with her meal. "Is there a grocery store nearby? I want to grab a bottle of wine."

"We'll stop at the Publix near my gym."

"I don't want our food to get cold."

"Should have thought to pick the wine up first."

"I'll run right in and back out. Do you have cups?"

"You'll have to drink it out of the Styrofoam cups at the office. It's how I drink my sodas."

"That's fine."

They got back to the shop and put their food out on tables in the break room. Laura got a lighter red wine since she knew Axel didn't have ice to ice down her wine. Then she looked around the break room and saw an ice machine in a new refrigerator.

"You didn't tell me you got a new refrigerator! I bought red wine because I didn't want to drink room temperature white wine."

"Sorry. Didn't think about it," Axel said.

He opened the food containers and laid the napkins out. Then he took out the plastic forks and the chopsticks.

"Do you need the forks, or do you use chopsticks?"

"Chopsticks. How about you?"

"Chopsticks."

"Where did you learn to use them?"

"Believe it or not, in prison."

"Really? I wouldn't think you had Thai or Chinese food in prison."

"We didn't. But there were some Asian guys in prison too and they taught me. Only it wasn't with chopsticks. Those could be considered sharp objects. I actually learned with plastic knifes."

Laura's eyes got wide. "Oh."

"Where did you learn?"

"When I was in college."

"Funny that there's a lot we still don't know about each other."

"We're still getting to know each other, right?" Laura asked.

"That's true."

"I don't even know your favorite color," she said.

"Green," Axel responded. "The color of trees and grass. Didn't see a lot of that when I was in prison. What's yours?"

"Hmm. I have lots of favorite colors. Mostly colors I look good wearing. So emerald green, royal blue, burgundy."

"You looked great in that navy blue dress today."

"You looked pretty great yourself."

"I'm glad we went to church. I want to start going again regularly. Promise me you'll go with me."

Laura sighed. "I guess I can't tell you no since I total y screwed up with you."

"One thing has nothing to do with the other, Princess. But I would like you by my side in church."

"I'll go with you," she said softly.

"Thank you."

"I should be thanking you. My mother will be delig ted. When I tell her you got me back to the church, she will welcc ne you with open arms."

Axel smiled. "Whatever it takes."

Laura pointed with her chopsticks to the little bit of l rown hair he had. "I like this."

"I don't," Axel said, running his hand through the sparse hairs. "My techs are teasing me about growing out my hair. I'm ready to shave it down to a mohawk and be done with it."

"Don't you dare!"

"I said it was my hair, Princess. You'll have no say f I decide to shave it all off again."

Laura frowned at the thought. "Since we are talking about things, we are learning about each other, have you ever made l ve in public places?"

"I got fucked in prison. That's as public as I ever wan to get."

"Do you like anal sex?"

"Do you?"

"I'm not wild about it but if you like it I would do it."

"Princess, I didn't like getting screwed in the ass in prison and I sure as hell don't want to do it to you if you don't like i . Why would you even ask me that?"

"I want to please you."

"If you don't enjoy it, how is it pleasurable?"

Laura picked at her food. Secretly, she was happy A el didn't like anal sex.

"Stop trying to be someone you aren't, Princess," Axe said.

"I'm not," she said. She played with her food some r ore. "You're right," she whispered. "I've been trying to be someon to everyone else my whole life. The good little Catholic girl to my parents. The perfect girlfriend to my gang member boyfriend. I've changed my skin to please every person I've ever known."

"You don't have to change your skin with me," Axel said. "Look me in the eyes."

Laura looked up to meet his blue eyes.

"I love you for you. As much as you make me happy or mad. I love you. Don't forget it," he said, emphasizing with his chopsticks.

"And I love you," she said, a tear rolling down her cheek again. "I thought I loved Julio. I really did. But I can see now that I didn't. I wanted to be in love with him to please him."

She looked down at her food, her appetite lost. She pushed her food away. She looked back up to tears in Axel's eyes too.

"I love you so much," he said, wiping his eyes with a napkin.

They both got up from the table and went to each other, kissing and hugging. Axel took Laura's hand and led her to his office. He quickly inflated his air mattress and they fell onto it without sheets or coverings.

They made love into the late night, but Axel stirred, and Laura awoke as well.

"Oh shit, you've got to go," Axel said, his voice husky with sleep.

Laura sat up, disoriented. She shivered. She crossed her arms across her chest. "I'm cold."

"Sorry," he said, reaching for his clothes by the air mattress. He grabbed some of Laura's clothes as well but was confused. They were his clothes, then realized she had come in some of his clothes. He handed them to her.

She quickly put on her panties and bra and Axel's gym shorts and T-shirt.

"Sorry," she said. "I just grabbed some of your clean clothes and put them on."

"Don't apologize. They look better on you," he said, smiling.

Axel walked Laura to the side door and looked out, making sure it was safe, then stepped out and walked her to her car.

They kissed at her driver's door and Laura got into her car.

"Love you, Princess."

"I love you, too, Axel."

Laura relaxed as the airplane lifted off from Hartsfield-Jackson Atlanta International Airport and headed toward Miami. She was looking forward to seeing her parents but was sorry she had to leave Axel.

They had become more intimate since that Sunday when they had the argument over her parents. They'd gone to church every Sunday and Laura found herself looking forward to it. She was pleased Axel didn't mind going to the Catholic church. She found the priest was delighted to have new, young parishioners.

When she landed in Miami, her parents greeted her at baggage claim. She hugged them both. Laura was pleased to see her father had good color after his heart attack and he proudly showed her the Fitbit she'd given him last Christmas.

She was surprised he was still using it. She thought for sure it would be in a drawer and his old watch would be back on his wrist. Then she noticed the display was blank. She sighed. She'd have to show him how to charge it again.

They chatted all the way to her childhood home. Laura could feel the relief come off her shoulders as she walked through the front door. She was glad to be back at home.

"Are you hungry?" her mother Carmela asked. "Can I get you something to eat?"

"I'll be ready for dinner, Mami, but I don't need anything right now."

"What about a mojito?" her father asked.

"Oh, I'll take one of those. I can't get anything as fresh as those in Atlanta."

Carmela went out the kitchen door and picked a couple of key limes off their backyard tree. She grabbed some mint, planted in pots by the kitchen door, on the way back into the house.

Laura sugared the rims of three glasses, then reached for the unlabeled rum in the kitchen cabinet. Their neighbor Diego Diaz provided moonshine rum. Diego had been a gang member in her late brother Rico's gang.

Laura sliced the limes while her mother muddled the mint. Laura dumped several heaping teaspoons of sugar in each glass, then took that same spoon and juiced the lime into the glasses.

Her mother added the mint and rum and she and her parents were ready for their first cocktail of the evening.

The day after Laura arrived, her neighbor Guillerma called her to ask her to go to the Miami clubs with her on Saturday night.

"I'd love to. Let me just clear it with my parents."

"Sure."

"And can we go shopping again while I'm here? I need some nice new dresses. I'm dating a new man. I'll tell you all about it at the club."

"Oh, I want to know more! Of course, we can go shopping. I need some new things too. Plus, you are fun to shop with. My other girlfriends get bored about halfway through. You never do."

Laura and Guillerma got into an Uber and went to some of the hottest South Beach nightclubs.

They first went to Story, a dance club. "Don't worry," Guillerma said as they stopped behind several cars lined up in front of the nightclub's doors. "I'll get us in. They know me."

Laura was in awe. Her friend could get them into one of the hottest clubs in South Beach? Laura suddenly had renewed respect for Guillerma.

Laura walked behind her friend, who strode into the club like she owned the place. Laura was glad she'd packed a "party dress" and her heels for the trip. She gladly wore them now.

The pair danced on the dance floor for hours. As the deejay was pumping up the sound, Guillerma leaned into Laura and kissed her.

The kiss caught Laura off guard. Guillerma saw the look of surprise on Laura's face.

"Oh, don't worry. I'm not bi, Laura."

"Hey, I'm cool with whatever."

"Are you?"

"I'm not bi, but if you are, I'm OK with that," Laura shouted over the music.

Guillerma pulled Laura into the lobby, where it was quieter. "Are you ready to leave? We could find a wine bar and talk."

"Let's go."

They ended up at Mini Bar at the Meridian Hotel in South Beach. There they could chat.

"Now, tell me about this man of yours," Guillerma said.

"I'm really into him. He's a mechanic, but he's the manager of his own shop. Technically, he's a client of mine, so I'm not supposed to be dating him. But I can't keep my hands off him," Laura said, giggling over a mojito.

"Oh, I totally understand. I love my Benny," she said, leaning in. "But I have a girlfriend on the side. I lied about not being bi."

Laura laughed out loud. "You go, girl!"

Guillerma looked relieved that Laura approved of her admission. "I met Alicia in the clubs. We don't see each other all that often. She's married, too."

"OK, I have to ask," Laura said, leaning over her drink. "How's the sex?"

Guillerma leaned back and laughed hard. "Oh my God! It's the best!"

Now they both were laughing. Guillerma leaned back in, so no one could overhear her.

"With Benny, sex is all about Benny. What Benny wants. If he's satisfied. He's such a man. With Alicia, it's tender and we make sure we both are satisfied."

Laura nodded, although Axel made sure she was satisfied, too. She felt bad for Guillerma that Benny didn't think of her needs.

They finished their drinks and ordered another. But around three in the morning, they both decided they were done for the night. They ordered an Uber and headed home.

The only regret Laura had about her night out with Guillerma was having to wake up early Sunday morning to join her parents for church.

Laura dragged herself out of bed and drank several cups of her mother's Cuban coffee. She put on a nice Sunday dress and headed to Sts. Peter & Paul Catholic Church, her childhood church.

Laura sat in a hungover stupor during the morning mass, avoiding her mother's disapproving eyes.

At the end of the service, she stood outside, blinking into the bright sunshine, and shaking the priest's hand.

"Laura, so good to see you today. Are you visiting your parents?"

"I am," Laura said, as she put on her sunglasses. She hoped the priest didn't see her still bloodshot eyes.

"Well, we are happy to have you with us today. Hope to see you next week."

"Sorry, padre. I'm leaving Friday."

"But we are happy to have her here," Carmela interrupted. "We will be back on Wednesday to clean Rico's grave and we'll be there for confession, too."

"Of course, Señora Lucas," the priest said in Spanish. "We will see you then."

Laura groaned inwardly. She knew in her heart she and her mother would go to the cemetery to clean Rico's immaculate gravestone, but she really didn't want to go to confession. The last time she'd gone she'd been pregnant and miserable. The whole experience had been traumatic.

Early Wednesday morning at breakfast, Carmela announced her intention to clean Rico's gravestone. She also planned to do it before confession that day.

Laura dressed in a light blouse and skirt but knew she'd end up sweating in her clothing. As she and her mother were cleaning the stone, Laura decided to broach the subject of Axel.

"Mami, I've been dating someone," she said.

"Oh Laura, I've been praying for you! Who is this man? Is it your friend you made the chicken for? Is he from a nice family?"

"I've told you about him already. But when I told you about him, I didn't really know him. I didn't know his heart."

Carmela paused, suspicious. "Who is this man?"

"His name is Axel."

"Axel? Is this the man who was in prison?" she asked, alarmed.

"Yes, Mami, but he's such a kind man. We are going to church together now."

Carmela eyed her daughter. "Really? A Catholic church?"

"Yes, yes. We are going to the Cathedral of Christ the King. It's a Catholic church, Mami."

"And he is going with you?"

"Mami, he wanted to go to church. He asked me to go with him."

"Is he a good Catholic boy?"

145

"He's Christian but he's not Catholic."

"Will he convert?"

"I don't know, Mami. We are just dating. We haven't even talked about marriage."

"But you love him?"

Laura scrubbed Rico's gravestone harder.

"But you love him, *mi hija?*"

"Yes, Mami. I love him."

"*Buena,*" Carmela said.

They finished cleaning the tombstone and placed the cleaning supplies back in the trunk of her parent's car. Then mother and daughter linked arms and entered the church for confession.

Carmela went into the confessional first, touching the worn wood as she entered the small booth.

Laura's mother exited after a few minutes and then Laura entered, touching the ornate carvings, worn down from years of faithful hands touching them. She sat down and the priest slid the grill so he could speak to Laura.

"Welcome, my child," the priest said.

"Bless me, Father, for I have sinned," Laura intoned. "It's been several weeks since my last confession."

Laura confessed to having sex with a man who was not her husband and not a Catholic.

"May almighty God have mercy on you, and having forgiven your sins, lead you to eternal life," the priest said. "Amen."

"Amen," Laura whispered.

"May the almighty and merciful Lord grant you indulgence, absolution, and remission of your sins," he said. "My child, pray the rosary for each of your sins and be helpful to your mother and father."

Laura said the prayer for contrition. "My God, I am sorry for my sins with all my heart. In choosing to do wrong and failing to do good, I have sinned against you whom I should love above all things. I firmly intend, with your help, to do penance, to sin no more, and to avoid whatever leads me to sin. Our Savior Jesus Christ suffered and died for us. In his name, my God, have mercy."

"Amen," the priest and Laura said together. The priest also asked her to pray to the Virgin Mother.

When she left the confessional, she felt lighter and knew she'd have to pull her rosary beads out of her drawer back in Atlanta. Unless she borrowed her mother's beads. Laura shrugged. She was not sure she wanted to do that. She'd rather use her own beads.

Chapter 18

Early Thursday, Guillerma pulled up to a warehouse unfamiliar to Laura. It wasn't the same one where they had shopped together last year.

"We're not going back to the other warehouse? I got some good stuff there."

"It got raided," Guillerma said. "You brought cash again, right?"

Laura nodded and patted the Hermes handbag she'd gotten the last time she shopped with her friend.

Guillerma went to the door and gave the password. Once inside, Laura knew she'd be buying dresses, handbags, and shoes. She was glad she'd packed light so she could fill her bag with what she now knew were stolen goods.

Laura giggled.

"What's so funny?" Guillerma asked.

"I probably am going to need to confess what I buy here to the priest back in Atlanta."

"You're going to church in Atlanta?"

"Yeah. That man of mine wanted to go and he didn't want to go alone."

"Is he Catholic?"

"No."

"What did your mother say to that?" Guillerma asked, rooting through racks of blouses.

"I think she's just happy he's an unmarried man. She wants grandchildren in the worst way."

"And you don't?"

"I don't really like kids," Laura confessed, pulling out a wine-colored silk shirt that she hoped would go with some cute leather skirt she could find while shopping today.

"You don't like other people's kids," Guillerma replied, holding up a blouse to her body, then putting it back on the rack. "When they are your own, it's different."

"That's exactly what my mother said."

"It's because it's true, Laura. I wouldn't put up with the crap my kids do and say if they weren't my own. It's because I can smack some sense into them. And I sure as hell can't smack other people's kids."

Laura laughed. Her arms were full of things she wanted to try on. "Where are the dressing rooms here?"

"Oh, shit. I should have told you to wear a bathing suit. No dressing rooms here. I guess women were stealing the clothes."

Laura arched an eyebrow at the irony. "Well fuck that. I'm not buying anything unless I can try it on."

Laura stripped down to her panties and bra and put on the two dresses and several blouses she wanted to try on.

Guillerma's eyes widened when she saw what Laura was doing. "Jesus, you look good. You must work out."

Guillerma stripped down to a one-piece bathing suit that looked a little too small on her. Both women tried on their items in one of the aisles, then checked how they looked in several full-length mirrors nearby.

"I want to try to find a black leather skirt to go with this blouse," Laura said, holding up the wine-colored shirt. "Be right back."

Laura disappeared into other aisles and came back to her friend holding a couple of skirts.

She once again stripped down to her underwear and tried on the blouse with one of the skirts, then the second one.

"What do you think?" Laura asked, turning this way and that in front of the mirror.

"I like the first one better," her friend replied.

"Me too."

Three hours later, the women were loading up Guillerma's car with their finds.

"I liked the other place better," Laura said. "We got champagne there. Here we got the stink eye from the security guards."

"I got the stink eye," Guillerma replied. "That one security guard was really checking you out. Didn't hurt that you were prancing around in your undies. He probably had to go in the back to jack off a couple of times."

Laura laughed. "Hey, I'm hungry. Want to have lunch? On me."

"Sure!"

"Pick your favorite place. I don't know the good places here anymore."

"Let's go downtown. Do you like Mediterranean food?"

"Love it."

"OK. We're going to Alloy Bistro. I haven't been in a while."

They made their way downtown to First Avenue and gave the car to the valet.

They were seated and Laura looked over the wine menu first. "Should I get a bottle of prosecco? You're driving. We could just get glasses instead of the whole bottle."

"Let's get the bottle. If we can't finish it, we can take it home."

"You can? We can't do that in Atlanta. If you buy the bottle, you better drink it all."

"That's crazy. Anyway, this is Florida."

Next, they got salads. Laura ordered the smoked fish and Guillerma ordered the filet. They split the grilled asparagus. They split a mango dessert creation.

The bill came to just over $200. "Please let me pay half," Guillerma said.

"Absolutely not. You saved me this much, if not more, by shopping at the warehouse today."

"You got some great buys."

"I really enjoyed myself today. Having lunch was the icing on the cake."

"I had a great time, too," Guillerma said. "I wish you lived closer. We could do this more often."

"My parents aren't getting any younger, so I'm sure I'll be down here a little more often. They want me to come home for Thanksgiving. I may bring my new man with me."

"Your mother will be delighted."

"She will, but I don't want to get her hopes up. We're just casually dating."

Guillerma snorted. "If you bring him to Miami for Thanksgiving your mother will be planning the wedding by Christmas."

Laura pursed her lips in a tight smile. Guillerma wasn't wrong.

Laura had called Axel every night she was in Miami. They even had phone sex a couple of times at night. Laura had to be careful not to cry out too loudly. She didn't want to wake her parents.

She also confessed that Guillerma had kissed her at the nightclub.

"She did?"

"Yeah. I wasn't ready for it."

"Did she give you her tongue?"

"She did."

Axel was quiet for a moment. "That's kind of hot."

"You are such a guy."

"And you love it."

"We can discuss that later tonight if you want to have phone sex."

"Fuck, I'm jacking off right now thinking about you kissing your friend."

"Axel! Save something for tonight."

"Maybe we should have phone sex now."

"My parents haven't gone to bed yet," she whispered. "I'll need to call you back."

Laura didn't want to hang up on Axel, but she didn't want him to have phone sex without her.

She called him back later that night, long after she knew her parents were in bed asleep.

"It's me," she whispered.

"I know. You come up on my phone, Princess."

"Are you ready for some phone sex?"

"I've been ready since you hung up on me."

"Sorry about that. But I really didn't want you to start without me. Or finish without me."

"What are you wearing?"

"I'm naked. What are you wearing?" she asked.

"I'm wearing the clothes God gave me."

"I've seen the clothes God gave you. I like those clothes."

"You were telling me about your friend kissing you. How deep was her tongue down your throat?"

"Pretty deep. I think she really wanted to touch my breasts."

"I want to touch your breasts."

"I'm touching my breasts for you. Are you stroking your dick?"

"You know I am."

"That makes me hot. I wish I was stroking it for you.'

"I'd like that. I wish your hand was on my dick."

"Feel my hand on your dick. I'm stroking it hard. I run my fingertip over your head."

Axel made a groan in the back of his throat.

"Shall we talk about me kissing Guillerma again? How she French kissed me?"

Axel made another noise in his throat.

"You're excited, aren't you? Me kissing another woman."

"Oh, God, Princess. I wish you were here. I wish your mouth was on my dick."

"I want to suck your dick. I'd be sucking it so deep," Laura whispered into her phone. She didn't think her parents could hear her, but she couldn't be sure. But if she thought about her parents hearing her, it made her feel more aroused.

Axel groaned again. "Sweet Jesus, I want you."

"I want you, too."

"Are you stroking your clit?"

"You know I am. I wish you were stroking it. I love when you stroke it."

"Oh, Princess, I want you back in my arms."

Laura couldn't answer. Her breath had become heavy.

"Oh, Princess, I'm close," Axel whispered. Laura could only moan her response. She laid her phone down on the bed.

Laura pulled the pillow over her face to keep from crying out when she orgasmed. She could hear Axel climax, too. He didn't have to be quiet, and she heard his shouting through the phone.

She quickly picked up her phone just in case her parents could hear him. But the house was still.

"Oh baby, I can't wait to be home. I'll be there tomorrow."

"Love you, Princess."

"Love you, too. Sweet dreams."

The next morning, Laura's suitcase strained as she tried to zip it closed with her new purchases. She planned to check the bag since she doubted she could lift it into an overhead bin.

She carried it down the stairs and to the trunk of the car since she didn't want her father to lift it.

"What do you have in that thing? A bowling ball?" her father asked, watching Laura struggle down the front stairs.

"I got so many good bargains when I went shopping with Guillerma. I guess I should have left some of them here. I'll be back at Thanksgiving. But I want to wear them in Atlanta."

"You should have given us a fashion show," Huberto said.

"I'll do that next time," Laura said, giving her father a kiss on the cheek.

"I'm glad you'll be back at Thanksgiving, *mi hija*. We miss you," he said. "Your mother misses you especially. She won't say it, but she does."

"Papi, I'll be here for the holiday, don't you worry."

As they stood at the back of the car, Laura said, "Let's say our goodbyes now so you can just drop me off at the airport. No need for you to park and all that."

"I'm glad you are coming home soon," Carmela said, hugging her daughter.

Laura hugged her father extra hard. She still worried about him.

Once she landed in Atlanta, Laura called Axel.

"I just landed and I'm about to get my car. Meet me at my place in about an hour?"

"See you soon."

Laura tried not to speed as she drove from the airport on Interstate 85, then onto Georgia 400. She took the Buckhead exit and tapped her foot impatiently at the traffic lights. She couldn't wait to see Axel.

She pulled into her condo's parking deck and saw his truck parked in the spot next to where she normally parked. He was standing outside his truck, leaning on the driver's door.

Axel walked around to her driver's door and helped her out of the car, enveloping her in his arms.

"Hello, lover," she said. "I've missed you."

She leaned in to whisper in his ear, "Let me show you how much."

Axel began to pull her to the doors to the elevator, but Laura pulled back. "I have stuff in my trunk. I don't want to leave it there. It's expensive stuff. I went shopping."

Laura popped her trunk and Axel reached for her luggage.

"What is in here? An anvil? It's heavy."

"Ha! My father asked if I had a bowling ball in there."

"Do you?"

"No. Just some new clothes, handbags and shoes."

"Because you need more of those. I've seen your closets, Princess. You'll have to get rid of some things."

"Bite your tongue!" Laura protested. Then she thought about it as Axel rolled her bag into the elevator. "I guess I could bring some of my older things to one of the consignment shops. I might get some good money for them."

"Like you need more money, Princess. Why don't you just donate them to women less fortunate than you? You know, the good Christian thing to do?"

Laura frowned. "Don't make me feel bad about wanting to sell my beautiful – and expensive – things."

"Fine. You do what you want to do."

Laura unlocked her door, and the couple entered her home. Laura took Axel's hand and walked him back into her bedroom.

Shortly after Labor Day, Laura suggested she and Axel go to a movie.

"I haven't been to a movie theater since before prison," he confessed.

"There's a movie theater in Buckhead that serves food and cocktails. You can get a burger or whatever and a soda. I can have a glass of wine."

"Dinner and a movie would be fun."

"And we need to get out more."

"Princess, we don't want anyone to see us as a couple, though, remember?"

"I doubt any of your employees would frequent this place. They are all at the tractor pulls, or whatever, on the weekends."

"What movies are playing?"

"You know I'd rather see a romcom, but there is a new Terminator movie out. I bet a lot of things blow up in that."

Axel smiled. "Well, you know I like movies where things blow up. Tell you what, if we go see that, we'll go another time and you get to pick whatever you want, even if it's a sappy love story."

"Deal. I'll go online and get the tickets."

Indeed, *Terminator 2: Judgement Day* included lots of things that got blown up. Axel got a burger, fries, and his soda. Laura got a grilled chicken sandwich with fries, but she also got a glass of white wine.

As they left the theater, Axel took Laura's hand and said, "That was fun. I like how they brought the food right to you. Now I don't think I'll mind watching a sappy love story."

Laura smiled at him. "I should get that in writing."

"Don't worry. I'm sure you'll remind me often."

"Maybe we can go next Friday night."

"How about Thursday? I'm going to open the shop on Saturdays until noon."

"You are?"

"Just for oil changes."

"When were you going to tell me about this? I need to do some press releases on it."

"I'm telling you now. I'm going to go in this Saturday with a few techs and see how it goes. We're just so busy now. I think I can justify hiring a few new techs."

"That's great news for the business. I'll work up some releases. Let me know when you make the change permanently."

"I will."

"But next Thursday, romance movie."

"OK. It's a date."

A few weeks later, Laura got an email from Bobby, letting her know he needed some press releases about another wildfire – the Snell wildfire. He wanted a release to let the public know Star 1 was not affected.

Laura picked up the phone and called him. "Is it bad out there? Is the winery OK?"

"For now, we are alright. I've already talked to Kyle But I've got weddings and things booked this fall and folks are getting spooked, calling Molly, and asking if they should cancel."

"I'm glad Molly is out there to help you."

"She's been great. I've hired her part-time while she's back in school. She works on the weekends when we have events and sometimes a few hours in the afternoon. She's a real go-getter. I'm glad you chose her as our intern."

"Send me some notes and I'll work up a few releases to send out to the media and we'll post the main one on the website, too."

"I am worried about all the smoke that's been in the air. It's not that bad here right now. But if the wind shifts and it gets bad, it will be bad for the grapes and the wine."

"What do you mean?"

"There's something called smoke taint, Laura. Smoke from wildfires ruins the grapes. No harvest, no wine.

"Why? How does smoke ruin your grapes?"

"Smoke compounds can be absorbed through the skin of the grapes. Smoke molecules bind to the sugars in the grapes and gives any wine from the harvest a smoky flavor."

"And that's not good?"

"That's definitely not good," he replied. "I harvested what I could, but some of the grapes were harvested really before they were entirely ripe. I'm not sure if I'll make wine out of them, or even be able to sell the wine. And I've still got grapes out on the vines waiting to be harvested, the red grapes. I'm worried about them."

Inwardly, Laura cringed. Not those wonderful Cabernet grapes!

"What can I do? Do you want me to come out there?" she asked him.

"No. Pray the firefighters can contain this and pray for rain, Laura. That's what you can do."

"I'll pray for you, too," she said, and she meant it. She'd be sure to light some candles at church on Sunday.

"Thanks."

"Stay safe, Bobby."

"I will."

Chapter 19

In the second week of October, Laura had a mild case of what she thought might be the flu. She immediately told Axel not to come over, since she was sick to her stomach. She certainly didn't want him to see her puking.

Within a week she recovered but still felt weak since she hadn't been able to keep anything down. She couldn't remember the last time she had felt so ill. Even though she was a grown woman, when she was feverish and sick, she wished her mother lived closer.

Axel called her every day, but it wasn't the same. She wanted her mother. But she appreciated that he cared about her.

She told him she finally felt she'd recovered.

"You're all better?" he asked.

"I am. Come over tonight. I promise I'm recovered. I'm not feeling sick anymore. Fever's gone too."

"You're sure?"

"But I'm not that hungry, so you might want to eat before you get here."

"I'll grab some takeout after work and come over."

By the time Axel walked through Laura's front door, he had finished off the last of his French fries. She gave him a deep kiss and could taste the salt on his tongue.

"I brought you a burger just in case you get hungry later," Axel said, holding up the fast-food bag.

"No French fries with it?" she said, smiling at him.

"Nope. I ate those. You wouldn't want them cold, anyway."

"That burger will get just as cold."

"I can eat it then?"

"Go ahead."

Axel reached into the bag, took off the wrapper, and in three bites had finished the burger.

"What are we doing tonight? Movie?"

"I think that is probably just my speed since I'm still getting tired. You know, I couldn't even drink wine. Everything made me feel sick."

"You *were* sick if you couldn't have wine."

Axel asked quietly, "Are you sure you're not pregnant?"

Laura looked at him, annoyed. "I am not! I am on the pill. Although last week I couldn't keep those down either, so we better use a condom tonight."

"Ah, shit. I wish you'd told me that before I got here. I don't have any with me."

"Not even in your wallet?"

Now it was Axel who looked annoyed. "Princess, why would I even need one? Once we started dating and you said you were on the pill, I haven't brought any."

"Check your wallet. Maybe you have one you forgot about."

Angry, Axel pulled out his wallet expecting to show Laura she was wrong. To his surprise, there was a condom wrapper tucked in one of the pockets of the leather wallet.

"How did you know? Have you gone through my wallet?" he asked.

"Please don't be mad at me. I wanted to see when your birthday was."

"My driver's license is nowhere near this pocket," he said, pointing to his wallet.

"You can look through my wallet if you want."

Axel threw his wallet down on the kitchen counter. "Princess, there are times I'd like to wring your pretty little neck."

"Come sit on the couch and let's watch a movie. I'll even let you pick one with lots of bombs going off."

Axel flipped through the schedule for HBO and found "Game Night." "Let's watch this. It's a comedy."

"I like Jason Bateman."

The couple settled in on the couch, but Axel wouldn't cuddle with Laura. She tried to hold his hand and he brushed her off. He eventually got up and got a soda to drink and returned to the couch.

"Are you just going to be mad at me all night?" Laura asked, frustrated.

"You violated my privacy, Princess," Axel said. "I had my privacy violated daily in prison. When I'm with you, I don't expect that."

Axel stood up and put the empty glass in the sink.

"I'm sorry," she said, following him.

"You are sorry a lot, Princess," he said, turning to face her. "You do and say things without even thinking of the consequences."

"I'm trying to be better!"

"Try harder."

Laura reached for his hand, trying to pull him back to the couch. "We're missing all of the movie."

"I don't think I want to watch it anymore. I think I'll just go back to the shop."

"Please don't go," Laura pleaded, grabbing Axel by the arm. "Just stay here. I want to be with you. We don't have to have sex or anything. I just want to feel you next to me at night. I missed you."

"I've missed you, too. I was looking forward to tonight. But now I wonder if I can ever trust you."

Laura felt tears beginning to well in her eyes. She knew how it felt to be betrayed by someone she thought she could trust. Axel's words stung.

"If you want to go, I won't make you stay," she said, releasing his arm. "I'm sorry I snooped. I was disappointed I missed your birthday and you never even told me."

"When's your birthday?"

"January 7."

"See? That's the way it's supposed to go. Not going through my wallet."

Axel reached over and hugged Laura, who began crying. "Hush, Princess. Don't cry. We're going to have fights every now and again. We're learning how to be with each other."

"Why does learning have to make me feel so bad about myself?"

"You have to ask yourself that. I can't answer that for you."

Laura just nodded into his shoulder.

"I hope you aren't crying that mascara into my shirt. Even with stain remover, I couldn't get it out of my other one."

Laura made a half-laugh. She thought she was probably ruining his shirt. "Quick, take it off and we'll put it right in the wash."

"Sounds to me like you want me undressed."

"Are you going to stay tonight?"

"I'm going to stay," he said, kissing her.

Axel then took off his shirt and started the washing machine while Laura turned off the television. Axel grabbed his wallet from the kitchen counter before joining Laura in her bedroom.

Laura could feel her excitement building almost immediately as Axel's fingers touched her collarbones. She began to unbutton her blouse and Axel's hands then slid down over the top of her bra. He cupped her breasts through her bra, then moved so his thumbs could stroke her nipples through the lacy material.

Laura let out a gasp of pleasure.

"Let's get you out of the rest of these pretty things," Axel said, unhooking her bra. He then unzipped her pants, and Laura shimmied to get them to fall to her ankles. She kicked the pants away.

Having fully undressed, the couple fell onto the bed, caressing and kissing one another. Each could feel their passion building quickly.

"Shit, baby, I can't wait," Axel whispered.

"I can't either. Get inside me."

Axel leaned over to grab the condom, ripping the package open with his teeth. He got it on and entered Laura, thrusting in her hard.

Laura thought she was going to scream her pleasure. She could feel her orgasm coming fast.

Axel thrust even harder as he came inside Laura as she dug her nails into his arms and shrieked.

He collapsed next to her, then rolled onto his back, panting. Axel reached down to pull the condom off and felt wetness instead.

"Oh shit, Princess."

Laura, nearly asleep, murmured, "What's wrong?" She then nuzzled closer into him.

"I think the condom broke."

"What?" Laura exclaimed, suddenly very awake.

"I think it broke. Jesus. It's probably been in my wallet for years."

"Years?"

"Well, not years. But at least a year. When I got out of prison."

"So not a year. It probably didn't break then."

"Princess, it's in pieces. Where's your garbage?"

Laura got out of bed and could feel semen running down her leg. "Oh no. I can feel it down my leg."

"You believe me now, don't you?"

"I'll take a pill right now. I took one yesterday and I'll take one now. I'm sure we're OK. I had my period last week while I was sick."

Laura went into the bathroom, took another birth control pill, then returned with her bathroom trash can.

"What do we do now?" she asked.

"I guess we'll wait to see if you get your period," he answered.

They both got back into bed, but neither one could sleep now. Into the quiet, Axel said, "Promise me, Princess. If you get pregnant, you will tell me, won't you? Don't do anything about it without telling me."

"I will," she answered.

Laura intended to keep her promise to Axel, but in the next three weeks, all she could think about was Star 1 winery. Several other fires had popped up around the winery.

She was on the phone every day with Bobby. He feared he was going to lose the remainder of his harvest to smoke taint.

"Do you want me to come out there?" she asked.

"No. Stay there."

"OK. Call me anytime you need me. I'm here to help you," she said.

Laura next called Molly to make sure she was OK. With winery events canceled or postponed for the time being, Laura tried to keep Molly busy with some other publicity work, so she'd get paid all of her part-time hours.

Knowing Star 1 was likely going to lose its harvest Laura alerted Kyle to have the restaurants that were a part of Seventh Heaven Restaurant Group in Atlanta to buy as much Star 1 inventory as they could.

Laura fretted about whether she should go to her parents' house with Axel for Thanksgiving. She'd already bought the plane tickets. And her mother would be heartbroken if she didn't go.

Bobby called the week before Thanksgiving to put her mind at ease. Most of the fires were now contained. She could sense the relief in his voice.

"How does the harvest look?"

"We're going to lose almost everything this year. No 2018 vintage at all. Even the grapes I harvested early don't look that great. I'm having them sampled to see if I can use them."

"Where do you sample them?"

"At a lab," he said. "But every vintner is testing at the labs, so there's a backlog. It will be a few weeks before I know for sure. I hate that I'm probably going to have to lay off some of my hands. They are hard workers. And I don't know what to tell you about Molly. I'll probably have to let her go, too." Bobby blew out his breath, then swore. "This just sucks."

"I've been trying to keep up her hours, but I don't know how much I can keep that up. Most of her work came from your events. Any idea when the events will start up again?"

"We can do some events once the smoke clears. We lost some business. Weddings and stuff canceled. I wish I had an indoor space."

"Why don't you ask Kyle if he'll do that for you?" Laura asked with excitement. "Your workers can do construction work, right? They could build out a space where you can host events inside. They could do the work. Then Molly will also have work. Win-win!"

"Let me look around and see where we might put it. Maybe we enclose part of our outdoor space and expand it out."

Laura could almost see Bobby rubbing his bearded chin in thought.

"Laura, that just might work. I'll get back to you."

Laura felt as if a weight had been lifted from her shoulders. Star 1 would make lemonade out of lemons and she and Axel would fly down Tuesday to Miami for Thanksgiving.

There was turbulence on the flight out of Atlanta. Axel clung to Laura's hand during takeoff.

"You're OK. I didn't know you were such a nervous flier," she said.

"I'm not. I'm hoping I don't puke."

"Here, take the air sick bag," Laura said, pulling the white paper bag from the seat pocket in front of her.

"Not helping, Princess," he said, then taking some smooth, deep breaths. "I'm also really nervous about meeting your parents."

"I'm nervous, too. But it's only for a few days. We'll be home on Sunday."

"Man, the airport was really crowded. I'm glad you said to go early."

"Well, you don't have pre-check, so I knew it would be a while to get through security."

"What's pre-check?"

"TSA pre-check. You get clearance ahead of time and can go through a shorter line."

"You have that?"

"Yes."

"Why didn't you go through the shorter line then? Why did you go through the long line with me?"

"Because I love you, you idiot."

"What do you need to get pre-check?"

"I had to fill out a form and then I went and got fingerprinted."

"Oh," Axel said. "I probably won't get pre-check then."

"Axel, I don't know that being a felon counts against getting it. You need to read the form."

"I'll look into it when we get back."

"Now, see? It's smooth flying to Miami."

When they landed, Laura called her parents, thankful they had finally gotten a cellphone. Her mother said they were waiting in baggage claim. Axel and Laura had both packed light and had carried their luggage on the plane. But Laura needed to know where her parents were in baggage claim.

"We're right by the doors," her mother said.

"Which doors, Mami? Is there a number above them?"

"I see the number three. Baggage claim three. Can you meet us there?"

"We'll find you. Can't wait to see you."

"*Te quiero, mi hija.*"

"*Te quiero*, Mami. See you soon."

"Do you always speak Spanish with your parents?" Axel asked.

"Sometimes. Most times. But we'll speak English for you. Promise."

"Unless your parents want to talk about me. I'm sure they will speak in Spanish to you, and I only know a few words from my prison days."

"Don't be so paranoid."

Axel sighed, knowing Laura's parents would speak Spanish to keep him out of many conversations.

Laura's parents greeted Axel cordially.

"You had a nice flight?" Huberto asked.

"It was a little bumpy at first, but it was fine after," Axel replied, squeezing Laura's hand in the back seat of the family's sedan.

"Laura tells us you are a manager of a car shop," he said.

"Yes, sir. That's how we met. She's doing publicity for the shop, Axel's Motors."

Carmela turned to look at them in the back seat, her eyes wide. "Oh! Laura didn't tell us it has your name on it!"

"We're hoping to open a second shop later next year, ma'am," he replied.

Carmela nudged her husband. "Two shops!"

"I only had one shoe shop," Huberto said, he said, looking in the rearview mirror and raising his index finger.

Axel looked at Laura quizzically.

"My father owned a shoe shop when I was growing up. He was the best there was," she said with pride.

"Now I know where you get your love of shoes, Princess," Axel said.

Carmela turned to look at Axel when he called Laura by his nickname for her.

"Why do you call her that?" she asked, angry. "Her Christian name is Laura. Why don't you call my daughter by her Christian name?"

"I didn't mean offense, ma'am. I think of her as my princess. I've just always called her that."

Carmela's face softened. "*Tu princesa?* Your princess? OK. Then that's fine." With that, Carmela turned back in her seat.

In a little over an hour, they arrived at the Lucas home. Huberto insisted on carrying Laura's luggage up to her bedroom. Carmela led Axel to Rico's old bedroom.

Axel was not surprised that Laura's parents put them in separate bedrooms. They were Catholic, after all. He did notice there was a Jack and Jill bathroom that led straight into Laura's bedroom. He hoped they might be taking advantage of that passageway.

After all the luggage and bedrooms were squared away, Huberto asked, "Are you ready for a mojito?"

Laura began to interrupt that Axel didn't drink when Axel replied, "I'd love one!"

Laura could not have been more surprised.

"They are really strong," she whispered to Axel. "It's made with hooch rum."

"Don't worry," he whispered. "I'm going to nurse that one drink like nobody's business."

"Good luck with that," Laura said, flatly. She felt sure she'd be putting a drunk Axel to bed that night.

Laura helped her mother make the mojitos, sugaring the rims of the glasses and juicing the limes with the back of her spoon.

Huberto and Axel sat in the living room, surrounded by family photos. Axel asked about a couple of them, especially the one that looked like an Easter photo, with the family dressed in their finery.

"Is that Rico in the photo?" Axel asked.

"Yes, my boy. I had hoped he would take over my business one day, but God did not see fit."

Axel was unsure what to say next. "Well, you certainly have a beautiful daughter. Brains and beauty."

"She tells us you have been in prison," Huberto said, cutting to the chase.

Axel tried not to roll his eyes. He looked right at Laura's father. "Yes, sir. I was convicted of drug distribution, but I've done my time and I got out early for good behavior. I'm not doing that anymore. It was a mistake and I admit that."

"*Bueno*. As long as you understand it was wrong."

"I do, sir."

Just then Carmela and Laura arrived with the mojitos on a tray. They handed them out and Laura, with her back to her parents, mouthed to Axel that she made his drink weak.

Thank you, he mouthed back.

Axel took a small sip, and his eyes began to water. "Wow. That's strong. I'm not sure I can finish this without embarrassing myself."

Laura smiled at him. Good job, Axel, she thought to herself.

"Oh, we get this rum from our neighbor. We're not sure where he gets it," Huberto said.

Carmela cut her husband a look. "But we're sure he gets it legally."

"Of course," Axel agreed.

Laura noticed Axel took very small sips through the cocktail hour and even excused himself once to get more ice and came back with half his drink and a lot more ice.

"I hope you like Cuban food," Carmela said prior to getting up to start dinner.

"Laura's made me a roasted chicken. She said she got the recipe from you. Was that a Cuban recipe?" Axel asked.

Carmela made a noise of derision and waved her hand. "My daughter barely knows how to cook an egg. It's my fault entirely. I should have insisted she learn from me. But she wanted to be out with her friends."

Laura could have died from embarrassment. But Axel responded, "Well, I remember how delicious that chicken was. She obviously learned something from you."

Laura could have wept. Axel was lying to her mother about her disastrous undercooked chicken and her mother was beaming.

"Well, my daughter is a very smart girl."

"She certainly is," he said, raising his mojito to Carmela, then taking a small sip.

When Carmela stood up to begin to fix dinner, she called Laura into the kitchen with her.

Laura gave a quick, uncertain glance at Axel. He simply nodded.

"Good, this gives us a chance to talk man-to-man," Huberto said after the women left the room. "What is your intention toward my daughter?"

"I love your daughter, and she says she loves me."

"You've been going to church with her?"

"Yes. The big Catholic church in Buckhead."

"*Bueno.* Do you plan to marry her?"

Axel squirmed in his seat. "Sir, we aren't to that point yet."

Huberto sipped the last of his mojito. "Can I get you another?" he asked, shaking the ice in his glass.

"Thank you, sir. I've still got some left."

"Well, I'm sure we'll have another with dinner."

The family eventually gathered around the Formica dinner table, refreshed mojitos at each place setting.

Carmela took her daughter's hand and her husband's hand before they said the night's blessing. "Axel, would you please do us the honor?" she asked.

"I'd be honored," he said, closing his eyes. "Oh Lord, we thank you for this day and the ability to gather before your table as a family. Thank you for this food and the hands that prepared it. In your name, we pray, Amen."

"Amen," the remaining family members echoed.

Carmela and Laura had prepared Lechon Asado, or roasted pork. It was a special dish often served on holidays, but Carmela decided Thanksgiving was a special time.

Axel continued to slowly sip his mojito, but Laura had added extra water to his beverage and not much rum. But she never got a chance to whisper it to him. In the end, there was slushy ice at the bottom of his drink, and he poured it into the sink as he helped clear the table.

Carmela and Laura shooed the men out of the kitchen as they put the dishes in the dishwasher and washed the pots.

When they came out to the living room, Carmela asked, "Are you ready for some coffee and dessert?"

"What do you have, *mi amor?*"

"Torticas de Moron," she replied. Carmela turned to Axel. "They are little shortbread cookies. They are easy to make. We'll have bigger desserts for Thanksgiving."

"Sounds delicious," Axel replied. "I'll just have some water with dessert. Coffee will keep me up at night."

"Very well."

Carmela returned to the living room with a tray of shortbread cookies, a glass of water, and a pot of coffee with cups and saucers.

She passed around the coffee cups and saucers. Laura noticed they were her mother's good china. Axel stood up to help, but Huberto waved to him to sit back down.

"The women will do it," Huberto said. "If we interfer , they say we are doing it wrong."

Carmela cut her husband a look but then went about] er work.

The four of them ate their dessert and made more sm ll talk before Laura and her mother washed up the dessert plates an coffee cups and they all turned in for the night.

Chapter 20

Axel and Laura stood at the top of the stairs, unwilling to part to their separate bedrooms. They hugged each other and whispered their love for one another.

"I hope you had a nice time tonight," Laura said. "I hope my father wasn't too overbearing."

"He was just being protective of his daughter. I'd have done the same in his position."

"Oh, God. What did he say?"

"Nothing awful, Princess. I guess we better go to bed before your parents come out and make me sleep on the curb."

"I guess you are right. I'll see you in the morning. Sleep tight."

"Good night."

Axel slipped into Rico's bedroom. He felt odd sleeping in what was clearly a time capsule. Nothing appeared to have changed since Rico's childhood.

As he settled into the double bed, he could hear a slight tapping coming from the other side of the shared bathroom door. He got up and opened it to find Laura on the other side.

Laura put her finger to her lips and led Axel into her room.

"I can't stand that we are just feet from each other. My parents are so old-fashioned."

"They just care about you."

"Stay with me tonight?"

"I don't know. They might hear us. And what if we fall asleep and they find the both of us in your room?"

"I'll set an alarm on my phone and you can leave."

"You aren't thinking of us doing it in your bedroom, are you?"

Laura's eyes brightened. "It makes me excited. I want to make love to you in my room."

"Princess, I'm not so sure that's a good idea."

169

"Don't be such a prude. Make love to me," she said, pulling him toward her own double bed.

She sat down and heard the creak of the old box spring.

"We'll get caught," Axel whispered.

"No, we won't. Not if we're quiet and careful."

"That old box spring is going to give us away."

Laura frowned. Axel was probably right. "What does your bed sound like? Just as squeaky?"

"I don't know. I didn't test it out for sex. I just wanted to test it out for sleep."

Laura stood up and took Axel by the hand, leading him through the shared bathroom and into Rico's old bedroom.

"Wow. This is kind of weird," she said, looking around and seeing all of Rico's old high school trophies and the tassel from his graduation hanging on the mirror. She hadn't seen his room when she was in Miami the last time.

"Ya think?"

She sat on the bed, which didn't make nearly as much noise as hers. She patted the place beside her.

Axel sat down and was impressed there wasn't as much noise from the bed.

"Wait a minute," Laura said, stepping back in the bathroom and returning with a towel. "My mother will know what we've done when she washes the sheets after we're gone.

"I think she's going to know anyway, Princess. These walls aren't exactly soundproof."

"But I want to make love to you," Laura said, defeated. She dropped the towel on the floor and sat back down next to Axel.

"Ah, Princess," he sighed. "Isn't there a chair in your room?"

Laura looked up and her face brightened. "There is."

Axel bent over and picked up the towel. "Come on."

He pulled her back through the bathroom and into her bedroom. He carefully laid the towel over the old wooden chair.

"I hope this will hold our weight."

"How are we going to do this?"

"I'm going to sit in the chair, and you are going to straddle me."

Laura shimmied out of her panties, then pulled Axel's boxers down. She took his penis in her hand and began stroking him.

Sitting in the chair, Axel leaned his head back and smiled. "That's nice, Princess."

"Do you want me to suck you?"

"Let's go old school tonight. I don't want to make too much noise."

Laura continued to stroke Axel until he was fully erect.

"Now?"

"Now."

Laura climbed into his lap and eased herself down on his erect shaft. Then she began rocking back and forth.

With one hand on Laura's hip, Axel slid his other hand under her and began stroking her clit. Laura let out a little yip of pleasure. She immediately clamped her hand over her mouth.

They began to breathe heavily. Their orgasms built slowly with the steady rocking of Laura's body.

As Laura got closer to orgasm, she began to rock harder, pushing herself as hard as she could onto Axel's shaft. He groaned.

"Shit, shit, shit!" he whispered as he came.

Laura kept her hand clamped over her mouth and made a little strangled cry.

Laura tried to untangle herself from Axel, but her legs were wobbly. She nearly fell onto the floor. Axel grabbed her arm before she did. They cleaned themselves and the chair with the towel.

"Goodnight, Princess," he whispered as he returned to his bedroom. He gave her a long kiss.

"Sweet dreams."

Axel and Laura's family sat around the Formica table in the kitchen, enjoying coffee, pastelitos — puff pastries filled with guava and cream cheese — and fresh tropical fruit.

"How did you sleep last night?" Carmela asked Axel.

Axel and Laura quickly glanced at each other. "I slept very well, Mrs. Lucas. Thank you for asking."

"What are we doing today?" Huberto asked.

"We are going to church," Carmela answered. "We'l clean Rico's grave while we are there. Then I must begin preparing the Thanksgiving meal. Laura will help me."

"When we get back from church, I'd like to introduce Axel to Guillerma," Laura said. She saw her mother's look of disapproval. "We won't be long. I promise."

The family went to church and the cemetery. When they got back, Laura texted Guillerma and she and Axel headed next door.

Laura was alarmed when Guillerma opened the door sporting a faded black eye.

"What happened to you?" Laura asked.

"Benny found out about Alicia," she whispered. Then she saw Axel. "Well, hello, handsome. I've heard a lot about you.'

"Oh? What have you heard?"

"Come in, and I'll tell you," she said, leading them back to the kitchen. "Want a mojito?"

"I'll pass," Axel said. "I'll take a cola if you have one."

"I'll take a mojito," Laura said.

"Thank God. I don't want to drink alone."

Guillerma and Laura set about making the mojitos. Guillerma poured soda into the third glass.

"So, you're not seeing Alicia anymore?" Laura asked in a low voice.

"Not right now. But we will see each other eventually. I need to let this blow over."

"If you ever need to come up to Atlanta, I have a spare bedroom at my place," Laura offered.

"I'm fine. As I said, I just need to let it blow over," she said. "Now, let's talk about you, Axel.".

"I'm not sure what Laura has told you about me."

"She said you were good-looking, but she didn't say how much."

Axel blushed a little.

"She said you own a service station?"

"I run it. My stepbrother – her boss – owns it."

"Well, you're in charge, right? He's not there every day, is he?"

Axel snorted. "He's never there. He lives in Texas."

The trio chatted amicably and after about an hour, the phone rang on the kitchen wall.

Guillerma got up to answer it. "*Si, señora*, she's here. I'll let her know."

"That's my mother, isn't it?"

"She says she needs your help with dinner for tomorrow."

Laura finished the rest of her mojito and held up the glass to Guillerma. "Thanks for this."

"No problem. I'm glad I got to meet you, Axel. Don't be a stranger."

"Thanks for the Coke."

The couple left the Diaz house and walked together just a few steps to the left and back up the steps to Laura's home.

"Did you have a nice visit?" Carmela asked.

"We did."

"Do you want coffee?"

"I'll take a cup," Axel said, raising a finger. "Are there any of those pastries left? They were really good."

"I have some left, but don't spoil your appetite for dinner. We have key lime pie for dessert."

"Maybe I'll wait for the pie then," Axel said. "But I will take some coffee. Need some help in the kitchen?"

"No. You sit with Huberto. Laura and I will make the coffee."

Laura and Carmela disappeared into the kitchen and Axel sat on the couch. Huberto sat in his recliner.

"You had a nice visit with Guillerma?" he asked.

"She seems very nice. I'm glad she and Laura are friends."

"They went to Catholic high school together, but I don't think they were friends when they were there. Laura was older, I think."

"Oh? When did they become friends?"

"Last year, after my heart attack."

Axel was surprised. Laura hadn't mentioned her father's health problems. "I hope you are recovered."

"Every day is a blessing," Huberto said.

An awkward silence followed. Axel began to tap his leg on the floor.

"Laura said you owned a shoe shop?" Axel asked.

"For almost 40 years. I had the best shop in Miami. I had to sell it when I retired. My son Rico," Huberto said, his voice trailing off.

"I'm sorry about your son," Axel said.

"Thank you," Huberto mumbled.

Carmela and Laura entered the living room with a tray of coffee cups. Axel sighed his relief that the awkward conversation with Laura's father was over.

After the evening meal, the family sat around the table having more coffee and the key lime pie.

"This is delicious, Mrs. Lucas," Axel said, popping another forkful in his mouth.

"I'm glad you like it," she said. "Laura helped me make it this afternoon."

"I hope she'll make it for me back in Atlanta."

"Well, we used key limes from the tree in the back yard," Laura protested. "I'm not sure I can make one this fresh."

"*Mi hija*, you can make one for *su novio* just as good," Carmela said.

Axel looked at Laura, not comprehending.

"She says I can make one just as good for you."

"I'm sure you can," he said, taking another bite of pie and scraping the last of it onto his fork.

Carmela and Laura began clearing the dessert plates.

"More coffee?" Carmela asked.

"None for me or I won't sleep tonight," Axel replied.

"It's an early day for us tomorrow, Laura," her mother said. "We need to get up early to start cooking. I hope you don't mind we're not having turkey, Axel. I'm treating you to a Cuban holiday meal."

Laura frowned. Why was she going to get up that early? She just assumed her mother would start the food and she'd get up to help later.

"*Si*, Mami," she said, knowing she was expected to be up. She also realized there would be no sex with Axel that night.

The family sat down early Thursday afternoon to a roasted ham, black beans, and rice, garlicky yuca, plantains with some dipping sauces for them, and homemade rolls. They also had mojitos. Laura made sure to make Axel's with more water than rum.

For dessert, they enjoyed Cake de Ron, a spongy rum cake made with the rum that Diego often gave the family. Carmela made Cuban coffee for each of them.

Laura and Axel climbed the stairs to their bedrooms that night almost feeling ill from having eaten so much rich food.

"My God that was good. I hope you can make some of that back home," Axel said.

"I've got horrible heartburn tonight," Laura said. "I'm going to ask my mother if she has something for it. Do you need any?"

"I'm good, thanks."

Laura disappeared and tapped on the door of her parent's bedroom. She went in and then came out with some heartburn relief tablets.

"Good night, Princess," Axel said, giving her a deep kiss.

"Sweet dreams."

"They will be of you," he answered.

As they sat down at the gate for their flight back to Atlanta, Axel said, "I feel like I walked through flames this weekend with your family. How'd I do?"

Laura held his hand. "They loved you."

"How could you tell? Did they actually tell you?"

"They didn't have to. I think my father really likes you. Why else would he want to talk to you all the time in the living room?"

"It felt awkward, though. And I don't know that he wanted to, so much as your mother kept insisting I go talk to him."

"She just wanted you two to get along."

"Almost made me ask you for a full-strength mojito."

"I don't think anyone noticed you were dumping the first one my mother made, and I made sure I fixed yours after that. I think the last ones I made you were minty sweet lime water."

"Thanks. I do appreciate it."

"I'm just ready to be home."

"Me, too."

Chapter 21

In the first two days of December, Laura realized she had missed her period. She wasn't alarmed at first. She thought the stress of her trip might have messed with her cycle. By the second week, she was worried enough to buy a pregnancy test.

"Fuck, fuck, fuck," she said as she stared at the second line of the test. She'd promised Axel she'd tell him if she'd gotten pregnant with that broken condom. But it took her to the end of the week to work up the nerve to tell him.

"I have something to tell you and I don't want you to get too excited," Laura began over dinner on Friday night. Laura was nervous and picked at her food, while Axel ate with gusto.

Axel looked up. "What?"

"There's just no good way to say this," she began. "I'm pregnant."

"That's wonderful!" Axel said, a big smile on his face. "We'll get married. I don't have a ring, but I'll get one."

"No, Axel. We're not getting married because I'm not keeping it."

Axel's face fell. "What do you mean?"

"I'm going to have an abortion."

"No! You can't!"

"I can and I will. I've thought a lot about this. I don't want to be a mother. It's my body and it's my choice."

"It's my baby, too. What about me? Don't I have a say?"

"You really don't. It's like you with your hair. I can ask you to grow it out, but even you said if you didn't like it, you'd cut it off again."

"It's hair, Princess. It will grow back. What you are going to do won't grow back," he said, his voice shaking with anger and alarm.

"I've already made the appointment."

"Please don't do this," Axel said, beginning to cry. "Please don't."

"I'm sorry. I just can't be a mother. I just can't."

"Why not? You won't do it alone. I'll be there with you. I want to be a father. It may be my only chance, Princess. Please."

"I'm sorry. It's my decision."

"We can raise this child together. Our child! Ours. It's not just yours."

"No," Laura whispered. She couldn't even look at Axel.

Axel stood up and began pacing in the kitchen. He felt his rage and sorrow build.

"If you do this," he said, his voice shaking, "we're over."

"I'm sorry, Axel," Laura said, grabbing his arm. "I'm sorry."

"You are destroying our love," he said, shaking off her arm.

"I can't do this. It's my body," she said, crying.

"Let me out of this condo, now!"

"Please don't go!"

Axel grabbed a kitchen knife from the counter and walked over to the control panel for the front door. He began stabbing the panel. At first, it didn't do anything. Then the hard plastic cracked. He kept stabbing it, his rage mounting.

Both could smell electronics burning. Then they heard the electronic locks release. Axel put his hand on the door handle and opened the door.

"If you do this, I'm never coming back," he said, weeping. "I don't know how I'm going to live without you. But I don't know if I can live with you if you do this."

"I'm sorry," Laura croaked.

Axel turned and left. He turned to look at Laura one last time as the elevator door closed.

Laura cried so hard she couldn't catch her breath. Even though she hadn't eaten anything for dinner, she rushed to the bathroom to be sick.

By the time the nausea ended, Laura felt weak. She didn't even want to return to the kitchen to clean up the food left on the table and the counters. She didn't even look to see if her front door was closed.

Her body felt heavy, and her head pounded. She took a pain reliever with a sleep aid and crawled into bed.

Laura awoke in a panic hours later. The nightmares of Julio had returned.

Laura sat up and rushed into the bathroom to be sick again. Naked, she laid down on the floor, the tile cold against her body. She dozed off on the floor, but eventually woke up, shivering.

Laura, on all fours, crawled toward her bed, pulling herself up and getting under her duvet. She wrapped herself in it, her whole body shaking.

Once asleep, Laura began to dream again, but this time she dreamt of her brother Rico.

In her dream, he was younger, maybe 11 or 12, long before he got involved in the gang. She could feel him hold her hand and brush her hair out of her face.

"*Está bién*, chichi," he said, calling her by his long-ago nickname for her. She could feel his hand on her cheek. "It's OK. I'm here with you. I'm always here with you. Let me stay with you."

Laura awoke with a start and sat up. "Rico?" she called out. "Rico?"

She realized she was alone in the bedroom. She put her face in her hands and wept.

Laura spent the rest of the weekend being sick and sleeping. She had more dreams of Rico – pleasant dreams of when they were younger – and in her dreams they were embracing. She awoke hugging her pillow tight.

On Monday morning, she got an early call from Kyle.

"Do you know where Axel is?"

"No. Is he missing?" she asked, worried.

"He's not at the shop this morning and his truck isn't there either. One of the workers called me."

The mole, Laura thought. But she was worried that Axel wasn't at the shop. That wasn't like him. He'd left her place Friday night, angry. Where was he? She hadn't heard from him all weekend, but his last words led her to believe she might not ever hear from him again.

She wanted to cry, but Kyle asked her to go to the shop and see if she could find out where he was.

"Kyle, Atlanta is a big place. How am I supposed to find him?"

"I don't know but I'm worried. Just see what you can do."

Kyle hung up before Laura blurted out that she was now worried too.

Laura drove down to Axel's Motors, unnerved to see the place where Axel normally parked his truck empty.

She went into the shop, asking the techs if they had heard from him. None of them had seen him since Saturday when he'd come in to work. And that was odd, because Axel didn't usually work on Saturdays, one tech said.

"How did he appear?" she asked.

"He wasn't his normal jokey self. He seemed upset about something, but he wouldn't say what it was," one of them said.

"Well, if he checks in, tell him to call Kyle Quitman. Kyle's worried about him," she said. I'm worried too, she wanted to say but didn't.

Laura drove back to her condo but was unable to concentrate. Where was Axel? It was unlike him to just not show up for work. What if his parole officer tried to contact him and he wasn't at work?

She paced her condo. She tried to eat some lunch but had no appetite. Even her beloved Cuban coffee wasn't sitting well. It gave her heartburn.

Several times she picked up the phone to cancel her appointment for the abortion. Then she hung up. Laura felt confused. She paced her condo some more.

Kyle called her Monday afternoon.

"He's at Grady hospital. Do you know where it is? He was in an accident."

"What?" Laura exclaimed. "I know Grady is in downtown Atlanta."

"Can you please go to Grady? He's out of ICU. He's in a regular room now. I can't get there until tomorrow."

"Of course, I'll go. Do you know what happened?"

"The police called me. He was driving his truck Saturday night too fast in the rain. He missed a curve and hit a telephone pole. He's alive, but he's pretty banged up."

"I'm on my way," she said, grabbing her keys. She could still lock her door the old-fashioned way, with her house key.

Laura went to the information desk and asked for Axel's room.

"And you are?" the desk nurse asked.

"I'm his fiancée," Laura lied.

Laura gasped when she entered Axel's room and he turned to look at her. His face was a mass of bruises, including two black eyes.

"What are you doing here?" he whispered.

A nurse looked up as Laura walked in.

"Mr. Lynch didn't indicate he would have visitors. Only 10 minutes."

Laura nodded and went to Axel's bed. The tubes and wires attached to him brought tears to her eyes.

"What are you doing here?" he whispered again.

"What's wrong with his voice?" she asked the nurse.

"It will get better. He was on oxygen in ICU."

"What. Are. You. Doing. Here?" he asked once again.

Laura began crying. "I came as soon as I heard you were here."

"Why?"

"Because I love you," she said, reaching for his hand. Axel tried to jerk it away, but his IV tube prevented it.

Laura sat in the chair by his bed. She stroked the back of his hand with her thumb.

"You don't love me. You made that clear," he whispered bitterly.

Laura shook her head no.

"It's done?" Axel asked, tears forming in his eyes. He turned his head so he couldn't look at her.

"I am going to cancel the appointment, Axel. I'm going to keep the baby. I can't lose you."

Axel turned back to look at her.

"You mean it?"

Laura nodded her assent.

"What made you change your mind?"

Laura smiled wanly. "You won't believe me, but my brother."

Axel looked at Laura, puzzled. "I thought he was dead."

"He is," Laura replied. She turned to see if the nurse was listening in. She was. "I dreamed about him all weekend. I dreamed about Julio, too. But my brother came to me in my dreams and said he'd always be with me. I think it was a sign."

Axel smiled as best he could. "I don't care what it was. You've made me a very happy man, Princess," he whispered through his tears. "Marry me."

Laura made a face.

"Don't look at me like that. Let's just do it. Let's get married."

"That's just the pain meds talking."

"I'm trying not to take the pills they give me."

"Why not?"

"Just don't want to. And I knew you how you feel about drugs."

"Axel, don't be stupid. You are in a hospital, not the streets. I can see it in your face. You are in pain."

Axel winced, tears running down his face. "Princess, I hurt everywhere."

Laura called to the nurse. "What's wrong with him?"

"Broken ankle, broken ribs, concussion," the nurse answered.

"And he's been refusing his pain meds?"

The nurse looked at Axel, then Laura. "His pain pills, yes. Let's just say he's stubborn. But he can't object when we give him meds through his drip," she said, pointing toward his IV.

Laura smiled, while Axel frowned.

"You be a good boy and take what the nurses give you. I want you out of here as soon as possible."

"You didn't answer me. Will you marry me?"

Laura nodded her head.

"I can't hear you."

"Oh, for Christ's sake I'll fucking marry you. Will you just shut up about it?"

The nurse's eyebrows raised.

"Sorry, sorry," Laura said, putting her hands up in surrender.

"I have a witness," Axel said, trying to move his arm to point to the nurse, but he cried out in pain.

"Can you give him something?" Laura asked.

The nurse left briefly and returned with an injection, which she put in Axel's IV. "This will take the edge off. It might make you sleepy."

"I don't want morphine," he insisted.

"Please give it to him. As his future wife and mother of his child, I insist. And since I'm pregnant, we better get married as soon as we can."

"Is there a hospital chaplain? We can get married right now."

"Absolutely not," Laura said fervently. "It must be in the Catholic church and my parents need to be there."

"I'm not Catholic, Princess."

"Well, you will be," she insisted. "You can take classes."

"That will take too long."

"I'm getting married in the Catholic church."

"Are you baptized Mr. Lynch?" the nurse interrupted.

"Yes, why?"

"Then you and your fiancée can be married in the Catholic church," she said. "My brother isn't Catholic, and he married his wife in the church. He just had to be baptized."

"Princess, you better pick out your wedding dress and we'll fly down to Miami as soon as I'm out of the hospital," Axel said.

"You better get a nice suit. You don't have one, do you?"

"Not really. You've seen my Sunday suit."

"I'll help you pick it out."

"Won't your parents wonder why we're getting married?"

"Once my mother hears she's going to be an *abuela*, she won't care."

"*Abuela?*"

"Grandmother. Once she hears she's going to be a grandmother she won't care why we're getting married, just as long as we are."

"Mr. Lynch, you won't be flying anywhere anytime soon," the nurse broke in. "You've got a broken ankle, broken ribs, and a concussion. That means no flying for now."

"Can we fly your parents up here?" Axel asked, then yawned. "We can get married here."

"I'd rather get married in my hometown church with the priest who knows me. Maybe we can drive down," she said.

"That's a long drive. And with my leg, I can't help you drive."

"We'll figure it out," she said, patting him on the hand again.

Axel was fighting the morphine but closed his eyes and began to sleep.

Laura stroked his cheek, then held his hand, careful not to disturb the tubes going into his arm.

"Congratulations on your nuptials," the nurse said.

"Thanks," Laura said, standing up and sighing deeply. "I guess I better call my mother."

Chapter 22

Laura had no idea what putting together a wedding entailed and quickly became overwhelmed. She'd never been to a bridal shower and didn't have the first idea of how to go about the process.

Carmela wept for joy when Laura called her to tell her she was pregnant, and she and Axel were going to get married. Laura told her she planned to get married in Sts. Peter & Paul Catholic Church in Miami.

Carmela sprang into action, securing the church's chapel for a Thursday afternoon in late December.

"It's the best I can do, *mi hija*. The priest said he is willing to forgo the pre-cana classes, but you will have to do them. You can do them in Atlanta at your church," she said. Then she whispered into the phone, "I told the padre we were in a bit of a rush."

Laura rolled her eyes. She could almost feel her mother hesitating over the phone.

"What?" Laura finally asked.

"He wants you to say three rosaries and pray to the Blessed Virgin."

"Of course, he does."

"Please, Laura. He is doing us a very big favor. Where will you get a dress? I have my wedding dress in storage, but I don't think it will fit you."

"No, it won't," Laura said, knowing full well her mother was not as endowed as she was. And there would be no time to alter the dress, even if it did fit. "Mami, I think I'm just going to have to buy a cream-colored dress. Axel is going to rent a tuxedo."

"What are your colors?"

"Colors?"

"For your flowers, Laura! Honestly!"

"Mami, I don't know!" Laura said, her voice raising.

"Since we have the wedding right after Christmas, why don't you do Christmas colors, like green, red, silver, or gold?"

"Green!" Laura almost shouted at her mother. "Axel's favorite color is green. My dress will be cream, so let's do green and gold."

"I'll get the ladies at the church to help me. Don't you worry, *mi hija*. We'll have the reception at the restaurant near the church. The ladies will help me with the food. They owe me after all the food I've brought to them over the years."

"I've got to call Guillerma to see if she'll stand up for me," Laura said.

Carmela made a noise of derision.

"Mami, please. She is my only friend in Miami, and I'd like her to stand up for me."

"Who is the best man?"

"Axel will ask his stepbrother, Kyle, to be his best man. He hasn't asked him yet, though."

"Well tell him not to wait. We don't have time! The wedding is less than a week away. Are you coming down for Christmas?"

"We will have to so we can be ready for the wedding."

Laura began to cry into the phone.

"*Mi hija*, what is it?"

"It's just, I never thought I'd get married this way."

"Laura, I'm sure the Blessed Virgin didn't expect she'd be carrying the Son of God, either. You have to accept this with a joyous heart. A baby is wonderful news. Do you love your man?"

"I do. With all my heart I do."

"And he loves you?"

"He does."

"Then you will be fine. You'll see."

"*Gracias*, Mami. For everything."

"I have dreamed of this day for a long time, *mi hija*. I just want you to be happy."

When Kyle visited Axel in the hospital on Tuesday afternoon, Axel told him he and Laura were getting married.

"I warned you not to get involved with her!" Kyle shouted, bringing an assistant nurse scurrying to Axel's room.

"Is everything OK in here? Do I need to call security?" the young woman asked.

"Sorry, no," Kyle said, trying to calm himself. "How long has this been going on, Axel?"

"Since July."

"And why the hell do you feel the need to marry her?"

"We're going to have a baby."

"You don't need to marry her, Axel."

Now it was Axel's turn to be angry. "If you think I'm not marrying the mother of my child, think again."

"I should fire you and her!"

"Well, you do what you want. I was going to ask you to be my best man, but now I don't think I want to!"

"And just who the hell would stand up for you? I'm family!"

"Well then start acting like it. Be happy for me. I love her and I want to have children with her."

"How does she feel about all this? Why isn't she here telling me with you?"

"I told her not to come when you are here. I figured you'd be mad, but you can't exactly hit me when I'm in this hospital bed."

Kyle turned and looked up at the lights in the room, then blew out a breath.

"Fine. Just don't say I didn't warn you."

"Hey, I know what I'm getting into. Laura can be a hot mess sometimes. She can be rude and thoughtless and speaks her mind when she should keep her mouth shut. Believe me, I know."

"I know she's not marrying you for your money."

"Not with what you pay me. No, she isn't."

"You're moving out of the shop? You'll live with her?"

"I guess I'll have to. I'm not all that wild about living in that concrete tower of hers. Reminds me a little bit of prison. Once the baby comes, we might have to find a real home."

"What about your truck?"

"Jesus. My truck. It's probably totaled. I'm sure the cops had it towed somewhere after the wreck. I don't even know where it is."

"How did the accident happen, Axel? Were you drinking?"

"Hell no. I was mad at Laura. I was going too fast in the rain, and I think I swerved to miss a car. I'm not sure. Next thing I know I'm waking up in the hospital with all these tubes in me."

"Why were you mad at Laura?"

"We disagreed about the baby."

"What do you mean, disagreed about the baby?"

"She was considering not having it."

Kyle raised his eyebrows, surprised. "And you convinced her otherwise?"

"I think she came to her senses."

Kyle shook his head. "Came to her senses. Maybe you should come to your senses," he muttered.

"Don't start," Axel said, angry.

"Let me know when the wedding is. I'll be there as your brother and best man."

"You keep calling me your brother. You know we are stepbrothers. Why the change?"

Kyle became emotional as he said, "When I heard you were here, in the hospital, and pretty banged up, I realized you really are more than just my stepbrother. You are my brother. You are my only sibling. I don't want to lose you."

Now it was Axel's turn to get choked up. "I don't want to lose you either." Axel took some deep breaths to steady his voice. "Does being your sibling come with a pay raise?" he asked, trying to lighten the mood, but as he laughed, he winced in pain from his two broken ribs.

"Take it easy," Kyle said, putting his hand on his brother's arm. "Let's just get you healed and out of here. Then we'll figure out the rest."

Axel was released from the hospital on Thursday afternoon, spending five days at Grady Health System. He had a boot for his broken ankle and pain medicine for his broken ribs. His face still displayed a mass of bruises.

He was wheeled out in a wheelchair and Laura and Kyle helped him into a large, rented SUV. They put his crutches, which he couldn't really use until his ribs healed, in the back seat with Laura

"I've rented a suite at Mandarin Oriental. I think Axel should stay with me for the time being," Kyle said.

"That's fine, but we need to rent a tuxedo for him soon," Laura said. "Our wedding is December 27. I need to get my dress, too."

Kyle cleared his throat. "I'm just going to say this once. You were not supposed to sleep with another of my employees, remember?"

"Are you going to fire me?" Laura asked angrily from the back seat.

"Wait," Kyle said, holding up his hand. "Let me finish. I'm happy for you both. I've thought a lot about it, and I think you two, in a crazy way, are going to be good for each other."

Laura sat back in her seat, surprised.

"If Axel is feeling up to it, we'll go rent our tuxedos this week," Kyle said. "You go get your dress. Are you going to a bridal shop?"

"I'll never find anything there in such a short time. I'm going to have to go to Nordstrom or Neiman Marcus and pray I find something that will work."

Kyle dropped Laura off in front of her condo. Laura leaned into the passenger window and kissed Axel gently on the lips. "Love you," she said.

"Love you, too, Princess."

Kyle and Axel drove to the luxury hotel making small talk.

"I really appreciate you letting me stay with you," Axel said. "I couldn't get around the shop like this."

"It was the only way the hospital would release you, Axel. I had to say I would care for you for the next week until your next doctor's appointment."

Axel rubbed his head, feeling his thick hair. "I probably need a haircut before the wedding, too."

"Yeah, why did you grow it out?"

"Laura asked me to."

"Oh, brother. You've got it bad for her," Kyle said with a grin.

"Yeah, I do."

"Well, let's get you up to the room and get you settled. You'll have your own bedroom and bathroom, but I can help you get around. I need to check in with work, too. Are you hungry? We can order room service for lunch if you want. If you're up for it, we can walk across to

Del Frisco Grill and get a steak tonight. You're probably tired of hospital food."

"It wasn't that bad, but it was kind of bland. Room service for lunch would be great. I'm kind of tired. But I'd like a steak, medium rare."

"You got it."

"Can I invite Laura to join us?"

"Do you mind if it's just us tonight?" Kyle asked.

"Sure. Maybe tomorrow."

"Of course. It's just…"

"No, Kyle. I get it. Guys night."

"Exactly. Maybe an impromptu bachelor party."

Axel chuckled, then held his side. "Whew. These ribs really hurt."

"No jokes. No comedies tonight. Nothing to make you laugh."

"Right."

They got up to the hotel suite and ordered lunch from room service, then Kyle helped Axel lay on the bed for a nap.

At five o'clock that afternoon, Kyle roused Axel from his deep sleep. "Axel, I made reservations for six thirty. Do you want me to cancel them? We can get room service again tonight."

Axel slowly woke up, dazed from his long nap. "What"

"Should I cancel our reservations tonight and order room service again?"

"No. I want a steak."

"Do you need me to help you get ready?"

Axel tried to roll over and sit up but groaned in pain. "I need help sitting up," he said through gritted teeth. "Oh shit. I don't have any good clothes for the restaurant."

"Don't worry. Laura brought some clothes for you. A couple of pairs of khakis and some button-down shirts. I've got a sports jacket you can wear."

"When did she come over?"

"She left them at the front desk," he said, picking up the new clothes. "Looks like she knows your size."

"She helped me pick out a couple of things for church."

"Church? She's got you going to church?"

"It's the other way around. I asked her to join me at church."

"Where do you go?"

"The Catholic church on Peachtree. She's Catholic."

"I think I knew that. Is that where you are getting married?"

"No. She wants to get married at her church in Miami."

"How are you going to get there like this?" Kyle asked, pointing in Axel's general direction.

"I have no idea. I can't help her drive. Plus, I don't think I could sit in the car that long," Axel said, looking in the mirror of the bathroom. "Jesus, I hope my face looks OK by then. I look like I've been in a bar fight. Are you sure you want to be seen at the restaurant with me?"

"Sure. I'll just tell them I owed you dinner after kicking the shit out of you."

"Don't make me laugh," Axel said, holding his side.

"Sorry. I'll help you get dressed and we can go. I'll ask if we can be at a table or booth in the back, if you feel uncomfortable."

"I do feel uncomfortable, but I really want a steak."

Chapter 23

As his wedding gift, Kyle flew Axel and Laura to Miami first-class three days before Christmas. He also had reserved a suite at a luxury resort on Key Biscayne for their honeymoon, but he wanted to wait until he gave the speech as best man to tell them.

Axel, Laura, and her parents went to midnight mass on Christmas Eve, stopping at the church door to speak to the priest.

"I'm very happy for you both," the priest said, taking Laura's hand and putting his other on top of hers. "We'll have rehearsal Wednesday at eleven, but I want to see you both in my office an hour before to go over some things."

"We'll be there. Thank you very much, *padre*," Laura said.

Axel shook his hand. "Thanks again."

The couple arrived at the church's office on Wednesday morning and met the priest.

"I want to talk to you about how you plan to raise your child," the priest said.

"We haven't really discussed…" Laura began to say.

"I believe our child will need a strong upbringing, and that will include going to church," Axel interrupted. "We've been going to the Cathedral of Christ the King in Atlanta. We like it there."

"Are you willing to raise the child Catholic?" the priest asked.

"We will talk about it," Laura said, trying not to commit to raising her baby Catholic.

"We would certainly like you to consider it. Your child will need a strong upbringing, as your fiancé said. You both are willing to take the pre-cana classes in Atlanta? That's important."

"We can take those. I looked it up on the church's website and they offer several classes," Laura said.

"Very good," the priest said.

"Do you have any questions for me?"

"How long is the ceremony?" Axel asked. "I'm pretty banged up from my car accident. I just want to be prepared."

"The nuptial mass is about an hour. We can get you a chair if you need to sit. You may have vows you want to say to each other. Have you written your own vows?"

Laura shook her head no.

"I'd like to say something," Axel said. "I'll keep it short."

"You want to say something? Now I'll have to say something," Laura said, annoyed.

"Princess, you don't have to say a word. Just look beautiful."

The priest looked from Laura to Axel. "Very well, Axel. I'll let you know when you can speak." The priest wrote a little note on some paper.

"Well, if he's saying something, I guess I will, too," Laura said.

"That's fine, Laura. I'll signal you to speak first, then Axel. Any more questions?"

"I think we're good," Laura said, standing up. She handed Axel his crutches and he stood up awkwardly after her.

The priest walked them out of the office and to a side door of the chapel. "I'll see you both in a little bit for the rehearsal right here."

The couple entered the chapel. Laura's parents were there, along with Guillerma and Kyle and various other family members.

"What are you going to say tomorrow?" Laura asked Axel.

"I'm not sure yet. I just have some things I'd like to say."

"I wish you'd told me you wanted to do that. Now I have to think of something."

"Princess, I was serious. You don't have to say anything. Not one word. I just want to see you by my side getting married to me."

The priest ran through the process of the ceremony, making sure everyone knew how they would come down the aisle, what they would say, and how they would leave the chapel.

After, the wedding party had a catered buffet at a nearby restaurant's private room. They would return the next day for the wedding luncheon.

As the rehearsal luncheon ended, Axel, leaning heavily on one crutch, took Laura by the hand and pulled her away from her family.

"I guess I won't see you until tomorrow," he said. "Are you ready?"

"As ready as I'll ever be. What are you going to do tonight?"

"Kyle and his wife and I are going to have an early dinner before we head back to the hotel. But don't worry. I won't be late tomorrow. I love you, Princess."

"I love you too."

Kyle, Amy, and Axel said their goodbyes and headed toward their rented SUV. Axel still needed help getting into and out of the vehicle, but his facial bruising was gone.

Laura had a restless night of sleep before her wedding day. She had to get up two times in the night to be sick. She finally dozed but woke up listening to the patter of rain against her bedroom window.

She rolled over and groaned, then heard a gentle tap on her door.

"*Sí?*" she called out.

"Are you awake, *mi hija?*"

"I'm awake, Mami."

Carmela entered the room and sat on the edge of the bed. "Did you sleep well last night?"

"No. And it's raining!" she cried.

"It's good luck for rain on your wedding day," said her mother, trying to console her. "Now why didn't you sleep well?"

"Maybe it's just nerves," she said to her mother. "I was sick last night."

"Maybe it's the baby," her mother said knowingly.

Laura put her face in her hands and wept.

"*Mi hija, no llores, no llores. Todo estará bien,*" Carmela soothed, pulling Laura's head to her shoulder. "Dry your tears. It's a happy day for you and this family. Your father couldn't sleep last night either. He's so nervous. He looks so handsome in his suit. He looks just like the day I married him. You'll see."

"*Te amo,* Mami," Laura sniffled.

"*Y te amo,*" Carmela replied. "Come, get dressed, and come downstairs for some breakfast."

"I'm not all that hungry."

"You are not eating for just yourself, *mi hija*. You are eating for *mi niento*," she replied.

"Mami, we don't know if it's a boy or not," Laura said.

Carmela gave her daughter a look. "I know. A grandmother knows."

Laura picked at her fresh fruit and barely touched her coffee at breakfast.

"Please eat something. Can I make you some toast?" her mother implored.

"Maybe a little toast. Maybe it will settle my stomach."

Carmela got up and made some dry toast and put it on a plate in front of Laura. "Dip your toast in your coffee. You'll need something to hold you until after the wedding."

"We need to be at the church soon to get ready. Guillerma is going to do my makeup."

"*Muy bien*," Carmela said.

The family returned to their bedrooms to get ready. Laura took a quick shower and put on a simple cotton dress. Her wedding dress hung on the back of her bedroom door.

"*Mi amor*, get your suit on and bring my dress," Laura heard her mother call out.

After they arrived at the church, Huberto held the umbrella for his daughter, then went back and walked his wife to the church. The sky began to clear. Soon a small ray of sunshine peaked out from the clouds.

"See, it's a sign," Carmela said, holding her hands in prayer.

Carmela, Laura, and Guillerma crowded into the small bridal room. All three wore casual clothes until Guillerma told Laura to put on her wedding dress so she could fix her makeup and hair.

Laura slipped out of her cotton dress, put on a slip, and then stepped into the cream-colored full-length sheath dress. Carmela attempted to zip up the back but had trouble getting it up over the waist.

"Ah! It doesn't fit?" Laura cried.

"*Cálmate*," Carmela said softly. "Lift the dress up a little bit."

Laura did as her mother said, lifting the dress up slightly and her mother zipped up the dress, then pulled it back down. The dress was very snug at the waist and Laura could see a very small baby bump.

Tears came to Laura's eyes. "Everyone will know."

"Don't worry. You'll be holding your flowers in front. No one will see," her mother said.

Carmela left to put on her own dress, uncomfortable dressing in front of Guillerma.

"Now don't cry or you'll ruin your makeup," Guillerma chastised, pulling a towel across Laura's chest so no makeup fell on the dress.

When Guillerma was done with Laura's makeup, she pulled Laura's thick black hair into a loose bun. Then she placed a tiara headpiece with a full-length veil on her head.

"Close your eyes," Guillerma instructed. She then sprayed enough Aqua Net on Laura's head to keep everything in place. "Don't touch your face and try not to cry. I did use waterproof mascara, but you never know."

Carmela tapped on the door and entered. She gasped when she saw how beautiful her daughter looked.

A few moments later, the women heard a gentle tap on the door. "Are you ready?" Huberto asked.

Carmela opened the door to see her husband, his thinning hair brushed back and in his dark suit. "*Mi amor!*" she exclaimed. "Are you coming for me today?"

Huberto smiled. "I'd marry you all over again. But today, I'm here for our daughter."

Laura could feel tears prick her eyes. Her father looked so handsome, so young.

Guillerma quickly gave Laura a tissue and Laura dabbed her eyes. Then Guillerma handed her several more tissues. "Put these up your sleeve, under your watch."

Guillerma changed out of her dress into an emerald-green dress with a plunging neckline. She then put on gold stiletto heels. Carmela made a face when she saw the dress.

Carmela had on a light gold mother-of-the-bride dress and sensible shoes.

Laura also wore gold stiletto heels. She took two steps and wobbled. She was feeling light-headed and unsure of herself. She'd never had a problem wearing high heels. Why was today different? she wondered.

Carmela was escorted to her seat by an usher. Guillerma waited at the church chapel door for Kyle to escort her down the aisle. When Guillerma and Kyle had taken their places at the altar, the wedding guests turned to the chapel door to wait on the bride and her father.

Laura leaned heavily on her father as they waited outside the door.

"Are you unwell?" Huberto asked, concerned.

"Just nervous, Papi. It's not every day a girl gets married."

"You are the most beautiful girl here today. *Te amo, mi hija.*"

"*Y te amo,* Papi."

Huberto gave his daughter a light kiss on the cheek and nodded to the ushers to open the doors.

Axel, in his perfectly fitted tuxedo, stood at the front of the ornate chapel's altar, his crutches nearby and a boot on his foot. An emerald green cummerbund was around his waist but was loose to keep from hurting his ribs.

He suddenly swayed when he saw Laura at the door with her father. Axel made a little noise, then swallowed, trying not to cry.

Kyle took Axel by his arm to steady him. Axel then nodded to let his brother know he was OK. Kyle took his arm away but moved closer.

Ivory-colored poinsettias, with gold glitter at the edges, an art project that the Sunday School children had done, lined the aisles of the church's chapel.

Laura held her bridal bouquet of cream-colored roses, baby's breath, and fern fronds tightly in front of her as she slowly made her way down the aisle. Her lips trembled as she saw Axel at the altar.

Much later, Laura wished she could remember any of the nuptial mass, but it was a blur.

When the priest turned to her and nodded, she had panicked. She couldn't remember anything of what she wanted to say. She simply shook her head no.

The priest then turned to Axel and nodded.

"Laura," he said, then had to clear his throat. "I con't want to marry any woman but you. You drive me crazy. There are times I want to kill you."

A small titter went out in the chapel.

"But you drive me to be a better man," he continued. "Today, in front of everyone here, you really are my princess. I will ove you until the day I die, and I vow before God to make you happy."

Sitting in the front pew of the chapel, Carmela dabbed her eyes as Axel made his speech, then saw Guillerma smirk.

"Ella es una puta," she hissed to Huberto sitting next to her.

"Shhh, *mi amor.* She'll hear you. She's not a … bad woman."

"Says you," she said in a loud whisper. "Doesn't she know you aren't supposed to look better than the bride?"

"She's certainly not prettier than Laura," her father said, emotion in his voice.

Carmela patted her husband on the hand.

When the ceremony was over, Carmela gave the evil eye symbol to Guillerma as she walked back up the aisle.

At the reception, Diego's illegal rum poured freely. The catering staff made mojito after mojito as the wedding guests celebrated. Cuba libres and soft drinks were also served.

Axel sipped his cola, while Laura sipped water with a mint sprig and a little lime juice in it. It was her version of a virgin mojito.

The luncheon consisted of empanadas, a tropical fruit salad, and a choice of Ropa Vieja or Masitas de Puerco, a marinated fried pork. Small buns allowed guests to make sandwiches.

For dessert, trays of flan and the pastelitos Axel loved were served. Axel took two of the pastries as the trays went around. Many of the desserts, especially the pastelitos, were made by the ladies of the church.

As the luncheon began to wind down, a drunken Guillerma stood up to make her speech. She raised her mojito.

"Laura, you did good. You've got yourself a real winner there," she said, pointing her glass at Axel. Then she sat back down and slammed the rest of her drink. Her husband Benny frowned.

Laura tried not to laugh at her friend. Nervous laughter could be heard from the other guests and Carmela once again gave Guillerma the evil eye.

Kyle stood next. "Well, it's hard to compete with that speech," he began, to heartier laughter from the guests.

Kyle raised his mojito. "Axel, my brother, has truly found a woman to be his match and equal. To paraphrase Guillerma, he got himself a winner, too."

"I want to tell you a story about me and Axel. Although we are brothers, we didn't grow up together. When we were younger, we spent about a week each summer together. I was always happy before he came to visit and sad when he left. We did the typical brother stuff when he came to visit in Texas. We fished a lot, rode our bikes all over, and told each other lies about girls."

That drew laughter from the guests.

"As we got older, we drifted apart. We didn't visit each other every summer. Life happened to each of us," he said. Kyle then cleared his throat. He could see Axel tearing up. "I want to say that after the happy couple return from their honeymoon in Key Biscayne..."

Laura gasped. She and Axel hadn't even talked about a honeymoon. The wedding was the main focus. They just assumed they'd stay somewhere in Miami for the rest of the weekend before returning to Atlanta. She could see the look of surprise on Axel's face as well.

"After they get back from their honeymoon, I want Axel to join me as a partner in my company. Axel, I know you are a hard worker and will learn quickly. And we can see a lot more of each other."

Kyle turned to see a shocked Laura. "And don't worry, Laura. You'll still work for me. I know better than to let Axel try to boss you around."

That drew laughter and applause from the guests. Carmela cried into her tissue and Huberto took out his handkerchief to wipe his eyes.

After the caterers cleared the tables, a deejay began playing the first two songs that the couple had requested for their first dance. Axel danced with Laura to Van Morrison's "Someone Like You," while Laura had requested John Legend's "All of Me" for her dance with Axel.

"We have a request from the father of the bride," the deejay said, as the Temptations' "My Girl" began.

Laura and her father swayed to the music before the deejay invited the guests to join in.

Then the deejay began to play music from Miami's nightclubs. Guests rushed to the small dance floor.

Guillerma pulled her husband Benny to his feet and began dancing up a storm. Just as Guillerma stepped back during one of the thundering songs, one of her high heels broke and she fell onto the floor, ripping her dress.

Carmela smiled. *"Buena. Ella se lo merece.* She deserves what she gets."

Chapter 24

Laura hated being pregnant. She complained constantly of indigestion and all the doctor's appointments she had as a "geriatric" mother. Geriatric! She had just turned 42 this year! That's hardly geriatric, she grumbled to herself.

Given Laura's petite frame and how tall Axel was her doctor decided to take no chances and scheduled a Cesarean section. Laura agreed. She dreaded the thought of labor. Although she didn't look forward to the scar.

Her surgery was scheduled for July 16. Carmela, who had never flown in her life, planned to fly to Atlanta July 10 to be with her daughter through Laura's first month with the baby.

Axel and Laura had chosen an airplane motif for the baby boy's nursery. Laura wanted to name their son Ricardo in honor of her brother. Axel could hardly refuse. "But I get to name our next baby."

Laura snorted. "Like I'm going to be pregnant ever again."

"Princess, you don't want our son to be an only child. That's a lonely life. I know that for a fact," Axel said. "He needs a brother or sister to watch out for in life, just like you had."

Laura frowned. "You seem to forget my brother didn't look out for me his whole life. In fact, his gang activity led to … unpleasant memories," she said. Laura didn't even want to say the word rape anymore.

"But our son isn't going to be in a gang. We agreed we'd raise him in the church. Hell, I even converted!"

"I don't think you are going to convince me to have another baby," she said adamantly. "Rico is going to be our only child."

Now it was Axel's turn to frown. "I really hope you change your mind."

"I won't."

"You are so damned stubborn, Princess."

Laura started to retort, but Axel's cellphone rang. "Sorry," he mouthed. "It's Kyle."

"Kyle, what's up?" Axel asked, moving into the third bedroom of the condo. That bedroom had always been used by Laura for storing things in the closet when she had no room in her master closet.

The couple had cleaned the closet and Laura had sold many of her older luxury goods to a Buckhead consignment shop. With the money she made, she was able to furnish the new guest bedroom with more than just the guest bed they had moved in there.

The original guest bedroom was turned into the nursery, since it was closer to the master bedroom, although they had a bassinet set up for the newborn once he arrived.

Axel came out after his call and said he'd need to fly to Austin for some meetings next week.

"You won't be gone long, will you?"

"No. I'll only be there for a couple of days. I'll be back on Friday. Then I won't travel until the baby is here."

"OK. I just want you home. I don't like being alone."

"I know. This will be the last trip, I promise. You want to cook tonight or get takeout?"

"I'll always vote for takeout. If I start the oven, sweat just pours out of me. I'm hot all the time."

"That's because this little monkey is keeping you warm," he said, putting his hand on her pregnant belly.

Axel had been busy since the wedding, too. With his promotion, Axel decided to hire a manager for the Lindbergh service station.

Then Kyle said he should look at opening a second shop in Sandy Springs. With Laura's connections to commercial real estate, they worked through brokers and the couple had toured properties together before deciding to buy one.

Axel began hiring technicians and another manager for that location as well.

As if he wasn't busy enough, Axel began taking an online MBA class through the University of Georgia, which had a program not far from their Buckhead condo. And it was their condo now. Axel had insisted he be placed on Laura's mortgage.

He worked hard, got good grades, and was well on his way to getting his MBA in 2020, so his partnership at Black Kat Investors wouldn't be questioned.

Axel left for the airport the next morning, undoing the repaired security on the front door.

An electrician had chastised them that the old wiring he found could have caused a fire. He replaced the panel with a new one and redid the wiring. The passcode was now 1227, their wedding date.

Laura could not get comfortable that night in bed. She missed having Axel lying next to her and no matter how she tried to sleep, she couldn't get rid of the heartburn.

She got up to take more heartburn medicine. She was eating it like candy at this point.

Laura tried to settle back in the bed, but baby Rico was being very active that night. She knew she'd never get any sleep. She sighed and got up to see what was on television.

Laura had long given up her beloved Cuban coffee in the mornings since it gave her even more heartburn. Plus, Axel had chastised her for drinking caffeine during her pregnancy.

No alcohol, no coffee, no sushi, or soft cheeses. No second pregnancy is what she told herself. If Axel wanted another baby so badly, he could have it.

By seven in the morning, she knew she could call her husband. He usually got up early when he was in Austin to get in a workout and then begin his meetings with Kyle.

"Hey," he said, when he answered the phone. "Is everything OK?"

"I couldn't sleep last night. Our son decided to do his gymnastics routine. He sure moved around a lot."

"I'm sorry you couldn't sleep. Can you nap later today?"

"I've got some press releases to work on for the winery, the restaurant and the new client you are working with, that software company."

"Be sure to take breaks and drink lots of water. You know what the doctor said about being dehydrated."

"I know, but if I drink one glass of water, I'm in the bathroom in 10 minutes. This baby is sitting right on my bladder."

"You're doing great, Princess. It will all be over soon."

"Says the man who doesn't look like he swallowed a beach ball."

"You look wonderful to me. Love you. I've got to go, Princess."

"Love you, too. See you Friday afternoon."

When Axel returned to Atlanta, he found Laura on the couch with a heating pad on her back, complaining of back pain.

"I feel awful. I can't eat anything, and my back is killing me."

"Have you called your doctor?"

"No. Why should I? I'll see her on Monday at my appointment."

"Just humor me, Princess, and call your doctor."

"I think you are being ridiculous," Laura said, but she picked up her cellphone and called her doctor.

After describing her symptoms and answering some questions, she turned to Axel. "We need to go to the hospital. My doctor thinks I may be in labor."

"But you aren't due until later this month."

"Tell your son that."

Laura was grateful she'd already packed her hospital bag. Tucked inside it was also a bottle of Star 1's Cabernet reserve, one of the last bottles made before the smoke taint ruined last year's harvest and no red wine was made. She was hoping they'd both have a small glass to celebrate after the baby was born.

Laura quickly called her mother to tell her that they were on the way to the hospital. "It may be nothing, Mami, but the doctor wants to check," she said, trying to reassure her mother.

"Oh, *mi hija*! I will go to the church and pray for you and the baby," Carmela said.

"I'll call you when I know something, OK? Don't worry."

"*Dios te bendiga, mi hija.*"

"God bless you, too, Mami. I'll call you soon."

Laura was indeed in labor, but it was slow. She hadn't dilated that much, and the hospital sent her home with instructions to time her contractions and to return if her water broke.

Laura said nothing on the way back from Piedmont Hospital to their condo.

"Are you OK?" Axel finally asked.

"I'm scared. I don't want anything to happen to my baby."

"Nothing is going to happen to him. We know what to do. I'll help you keep track."

"Should I call my mother? I don't want to worry her."

"You'd better call her because she's already worried and praying."

Laura called her mother, who picked up the house phone after the first ring.

"Is the baby OK?" Carmela asked in rapid Spanish.

"He's fine, but he may be here sooner than we think. Can you change your flight and come up?"

Laura tried to keep the panic and worry out of her voice. But right now, she wanted her mother.

Carmela hesitated. She had no idea how to change a flight and told Laura so.

"Mami, you need to call the airline and see if you can change the flight."

"Tell her I'll do it," Axel said.

"Axel says he'll call and change it."

"*Gracias, mi hija. Te casaste con un buen hombre.*"

"I know I married a good man, Mami."

Axel smiled. He then called the airline and canceled Carmela's original flight. Instead, he booked Huberto and Carmela on a first-class flight to Atlanta the next day.

He told Laura what he'd done, and Laura looked relieved. "Thank you."

"Do you think they'll want to stay here with us, or should I get a hotel room for them? Kyle likes the Mandarin Oriental, although it's not that anymore. It's something else."

"I think it's the Waldorf Astoria now," Laura said. "I'm sure it's just as nice. I'll call Mami now and tell them to pack their bags. I'm not sure how long my father will want to stay. I'll ask if they want to stay with us or at the hotel, but I bet our guest bedroom will be occupied this week."

Laura's labor stopped in the night and her doctor told her to get to the hospital immediately. The baby could be in distress.

Laura panicked. Axel drove back to Piedmont Hospital and ordered a car service to pick up Laura's parents the next day.

Hooked up to a fetal monitor, Laura could not keep the worry from her face.

"It's going to be OK, Princess," Axel said, holding her hand.

The doctor appeared and told the couple they were going to do a C-section immediately. Had Laura eaten anything within the past 24 hours?

No, she confirmed. The thought of food made her nauseated.

Laura was wheeled into surgery with Axel holding her hand.

In the early morning hours of June 30, Ricardo Alan Lynch arrived at Piedmont Hospital. At first, Laura didn't hear him cry and began weeping, thinking he had died.

Then Rico let out a howl and Laura's tears of sorrow turned to tears of joy.

The nurse placed the cleaned baby, with his full head of black hair, on Laura's chest and Axel began to cry as well. Laura thought her heart would break with happiness.

She now understood what her mother had meant about having your own child. She loved her new son more than her own life. Looking into his face, she knew she would do anything for him.

Shortly after they arrived from the airport, Carmela and Huberto hurried into Laura's labor and delivery room. Laura had just finished feeding her son and cradled him in her arms.

Carmela took one look at her grandson and her hands flew to her face.

"*Mio Dio*! He looks just like Rico did as a baby," her mother cried, crossing herself before kissing the baby on the head, then smoothing back his hair. Then she kissed her daughter on the forehead.

Carmela stood at the foot of Laura's hospital bed, took her rosary beads out of her pocket, and began praying in Spanish to the Blessed Virgin.

When Carmela was finished, she pulled a second set out and gave it to Laura. "Father Luis blessed these for Rico," her mother said.

Huberto clapped Axel on the back and handed him a Cuban cigar.

"*Ese es mi nieto*," Huberto said, emotion in his voice. "My grandson!"

Full Throttle

In that moment, Laura looked upon the face of her newborn son, making little suckling noises with his mouth, and knew — God willing — he would have siblings.

Made in the USA
Columbia, SC
27 July 2024